The Russian Jerusalem

ELAINE FEINSTEIN was educated at Newnham College, Cambridge. She has worked as a university lecturer, a subeditor, and a freelance journalist. Since 1980, when she was made a Fellow of the Royal Society of Literature, she has lived as a full-time writer. In 1990, she received a Cholmondeley Award for Poetry, and was given an Honorary D.Litt from the University of Leicester. Her versions of the poems of Marina Tsvetaeva – for which she received three translation awards from the Arts Council – were first published in 1971. She has written fourteen novels, many radio plays, television dramas, and five biographies, including the critically acclaimed *A Captive Lion: the Life of Marina Tsvetaeva* (1987) and *Pushkin* (1998). *Ted Hughes: The Life of a Poet* (2001), was shortlisted for the biennial Marsh Biography Prize. Her biography of Anna Akhmatova, *Anna of all the Russias* was published in 2005. Elaine Feinstein has travelled extensively, not only to read her work at festivals across the world, but to be Writer in Residence for the British Council, first in Singapore, and then in Tromsø, Norway. She was a Rockefeller Foundation Fellow at Bellagio in 1998. Her poems have been widely anthologised. Her *Collected Poems and Translations* (2002) was a Poetry Book Society Special Commendation. She has served as a judge for the Gregory Awards, the Independent Foreign Fiction Award, the Costa Poetry Prize and the Rossica Award for Literature translated from Russian, and in 1995 was chairman of the judges for the T.S. Eliot Prize.

ELAINE FEINSTEIN

The Russian Jerusalem

CARCANET

Acknowledgements

The author is grateful to Arts Council England, whose generosity made this book possible. She thanks Judith Willson for the care she has taken throughout the production.

First published in Great Britain in 2008 by
Carcanet Press Limited
Alliance House
Cross Street
Manchester M2 7AQ

The illustrations are taken from drawings by William Kermode (1895–1959)
in M. Ilin, *Moscow Has a Plan: A Soviet Primer*, trans. G.S. Counts and
N.P. Lodge (London, 1931). Every effort has been made to trace the
copyright-holder. The publishers regret that this has proved impossible,
but would be pleased to include appropriate acknowledgement in
a future edition if notified by the copyright-holder.

A CIP catalogue record for this book is available from the British Library
ISBN 978 1 85754 910 2

The publisher acknowledges financial assistance from Arts Council England

Typeset by XL Publishing Services, Tiverton
Printed and bound in England by SRP Ltd, Exeter

Contents

'All poets are Jews.'

Marina Tsvetaeva

I

They were almost unaware of the poetry they moved in.
　　It was like birdsong in a garden:
– ash tree clarity, sycamore vision –

and St Petersburg itself an elegant mirage,
　　a festival of peace time soldiers,
ball dresses and marble palaces.

Among so many Russians, one was an upstart,
　　inwardly awkward, writing as he walked,
a white-knobbed stick his Jewish crosier, but

sometimes unfortunate people are very happy.
　　He dreamed of the South with a copper moon,
blue-eyed dragonflies, and an Easter foolery

of sugared almonds and fallen tamarisk leaves
　　while in Kiev a hundred old men
in striped *talisim* sat at benches in grief.

All that is left now of that Silver Age
　　is space and stars and a few singers
who have learnt the sad language of goodbyes.

2 St Petersburg 2005

That September, St Petersburg was a city of freezing rain, blown horizontally into the eyes of anyone walking the streets in the direction of the sea. And St Petersburg is a landscape of sea and sky. When it rains, the brown skies and wet streets are continuous.

I'd rented a flat just off Sadovaya Square in a poor area of the inner city. The Square itself was filled with cranes and boarded up with planks. Taxis brought me through an archway into a dark courtyard with unexpected holes going down to the plumbing. There might be sable coats and French *haute couture* in the glass-fronted shops on Nevsky Prospekt, but the streets just behind were still open to the sewerage.

The flat, on the ground floor of a stucco building pitted by weather, was owned by a molecular biologist. He had a PhD from a university in the States, and a research job in an Institute of Biochemistry, but his pay was sporadic and he lived on the rent from the flat and his wife's classes in psychotherapy. These last were eagerly sought in post-Communist Russia. She used one of the rooms by arrangement three times a week, and there were tapes of sixties American folk music, and a sense of alternative hippy culture.

Handing over the keys to me, he insisted the flat had to be locked and chained even when I was inside it. Burglaries are understandably commonplace, though I'd been assured by a laconic friend as I set out for St Petersburg, 'There's much less street crime. The Mafia has got its act together.'

4

It was a spacious flat, but very cold because central heating remains under the control of the municipal authorities, who turn it on every year at the appointed date, regardless of the weather. The flat's only other form of heating was a single bar electric heater. In 1998, when my husband was still alive and travelling with me, he lit the flames of the gas cooker in the kitchen to save us from hypothermia. Now he lies buried in Willesden Green cemetery.

For the most part, the tenants round the courtyard were Korean. At the end of the street, wooden booths sold bread, and milk. Old women in bulky clothes with their hands in mittens weighed and sliced sausages. They also sold drinking water in unlabelled polystyrene containers the size of petrol cans. This I did not trust and found it worth walking round the square to a small supermarket to buy bottled water, which was necessary even for brushing my teeth. The liquid which comes out of St Petersburg taps has a nasty bug, even if residents have become immune to it.

Once, on an overnight train to Moscow, two rumbustious, vodka-drinking industrial chemists explained the presence of the famous bug. The source of St Petersburg water remains as clear and pure as a Highland spring. It is the filtering mechanism that is infected: a telling image for that network of hands – Joint Enterprise, old apparatchik or opportunist – whose greed has polluted the Russian dream of a Western free society.

This remains Peter's city, built on the tears and the corpses of his slave workers, who dragged earth on old sacks and bark matting so that the grand Rastrelli palaces could glow in the water of the River Neva. It's also the city of Pushkin's Queen of Spades, where poor Herman stood looking up at the Countess's window while large flakes of wet snow fell on his greatcoat; Akhmatova's city of granite and disaster; the Petropolis of Mandelstam's dreams, where the streetlights look as yellow as drops of cod liver oil in the sleety mist.

It was never my city, though I had visited many times. My family never lived here. They moved from the *stetls* of Belorus in the last decades of the nineteenth century to find homes in Britain, Canada or Latin America or went south to Odessa, a city of acacia trees and street cafes, dumplings and seed bread where half the population were Jews, many with a Russian education.

So what draws me to this city where only wealthy Jews were allowed to live under the Tsar, and where they suffered like everyone through civil war, Stalin's Terror and Hitler's siege? Not the glories of the Hermitage, though no visitor could reach the end of the European art collected there: the Matisses, the Impressionists, the paintings stolen from German collectors. Not the dark green painted stucco of the Winter Palace either, nor the golden curlicues on the staircases within, the marble columns, the jewel box ceilings. Not the great statue of Peter the Great on the Embankment, not the golden dome of St Isaac's.

I am here for ghosts.

Below street level on Mikhailovskoye Square, the legendary cellar of The Stray Dog has opened once again, though for tourists now, not the great spirits of the Silver Age who once gathered there after the theatres closed and often stayed talking until dawn. To reach The Stray Dog, you still have to descend a narrow stone staircase, and enter a low doorway. The windows of the café are blocked even now, as if to keep out the everyday world, but these days the walls and ceilings of low, curving plaster are no longer painted with flowers and birds in brilliant colours.

A blink, and Osip Mandelstam, barely twenty years old is there, with his long lashes, and a lily of the valley in his buttonhole, sitting at a side table with Akhmatova, a melancholy young beauty with a black agate necklace. Princess Salomea Andronikova, his Solominka, sits at the same table. They are drinking chilled Chablis and eating white *bulka* rather than black Russian *khleb*.

Thirty years ago I was ensnared by the dangerous glamour of those ghosts, a glamour much to be wished for if you come from a town in the English Midlands. My own roots always drew nourishment from elsewhere, and I grew up passionately aware of it.

My parents came from very different families, but both of my grandfathers were Russian Jews. My mother's father Solomon was a glass merchant; small, sandy haired and clean shaven, with starched triangles to his white collars, and a single rose-cut stone in his tiepin. He was a crabby man, but an able one; his sons went to Cambridge, and changed the family name to Compton as they entered the English establishment.

It is my other grandfather I remember, however. Among my earliest memories of our little house in Groby Road, Leicester, is a large ginger-bearded man seen through the slats of my cot. He had blue eyes with deep laughter lines, and I never saw him anything but cheerful. I thought of Menachem Mendl as my Russian grandfather.

He was not a fastidious man. Perhaps he wore a suit when he went to the synagogue, but I don't remember him doing so. His cardigans sagged at the back and he smelled of peppermint and snuff. His large yellow handkerchiefs were chosen to disguise that habit. He left his cigars half-smoked in ashtrays all round the house. My mother folded her lips tightly as she collected them up. When he drank lemon tea from a glass in a metal holder, holding a lump of sugar in his mouth the while, he said it was always drunk so in *der heim*. I was not sure then what country he came from, but he was old, had a strong accent and his gestures were not English. I was taught to call him *Zaida*, not Grandpa.

And I liked his stories. When I sat on his knee, he told me about scholars and dreamers, and young men and women dancing together in the forests. He had lost the top joint of one of his fingers, and showed me the stump of his smooth, unmarked knuckle which had healed perfectly. He was a dreamer, too absent-minded to be left in charge of a circular saw.

About his own childhood Zaida spoke little, but he had lived for a time in Odessa, and that he described with love: the bustle in the wide streets, the music everywhere, and the liveliness of the Jews.

When I was eight, my father bought a plot of land in Elmsleigh Avenue and built a big house on it. It was a leafy bit of Leicester, a suburb in the south of the city, where neighbours dressed quietly. He was proud of the oak floors and doors of solid wood. Each room had its own colours. The dining room had russet tones, picked up in the huge stone fireplace. Zaida lived in the large front room with a bay window and delicate lilac colouring, sleeping in a wide put-u-up bed, opened out for him by my father at night and covered with a rug of patchwork squares of thick velvet during the day.

Sometimes Zaida lamented the absence of Jews in Leicester. Certainly there were few living nearby, though the war brought Jewish refugees, market traders from

London, and Jewish servicemen from America, and my father invited them to our home for meals.

The adventures of my forebears are not my only connection to Russia, however. For nearly forty years I have been infatuated with their poets, their very being as much as their genius. It is something to do with the love between friends that I first understood reading Nadezhda Mandelstam's *Hope Against Hope*. Poetry underpinned that friendship, and I found it enviable. There is an intensity to Russian friendship which is stronger than the passion of sexual love.

Long before I put a foot on Russian soil, I had close Russian friends, first among them Masha Enzensberger, a white-skinned beauty with high Tatar cheekbones and blue eyes glittering like frozen sea, recently separated from the poet Hans Magnus. We met in the bar of the University of Essex, and talked through my version of Tsvetaeva's 'Attempt At Jealousy', a poem we both had reason to treasure. Masha was unhappy in England, homesick for Russia, yet unwilling to spend the rest of her life in the Soviet Union. She resembled her father, the novelist Fadeev, whom she had met only rarely; her mother was the poet Margarita Aliger, then well-placed in Moscow. Masha travelled between Moscow and Cambridge, where for a time she had a Fellowship at King's College. There she entertained lavishly, striking a glass to command Russian-style toasts from sheepish Cambridge dons. For me, she was the voice of Marina Tsvetaeva's poetry, which she read – while keeping her name out of the *Radio Times* – in a series of radio programmes I put together in the 1970s. We often shared our troubles, but she was more deeply troubled than I knew. I saw her last in a Moscow of brown streets, puddles and people still shaking with euphoria after defeating the military coup in 1991. She had been among the women who held hands to confront the tanks. The victory excited her so much she was unable to sleep. A few days after she returned to London, she took her own life.

Through Masha, I met many Russians, including Princess Salomea Andronikova, Mandelstam's Solominka, herself at that time living with Anna Kallin in a Chelsea flat. The princess was still beautiful, and I admired her poise. I remember only that the china was pretty and that Salomea, even in her seventies, still looked exquisite. I imagined it was her husband, the banker Halpern, who had left her so well provided for, but it turned out the flat was the gift of Sir Isaiah Berlin. I was far closer to Vera Traill, whose rackety life had stranded her in Cambridge in her sixties. She was the daughter of Guchkov, a great industrialist, who was a member of Russia's short-lived Duma in 1917. In her childhood, she remembered being driven around in one of the few cars Moscow could boast before the First World War.

Masha disapproved of Vera profoundly. Rumour had it that she had been, and perhaps still was, an agent of the NKVD. I was more intrigued than disapproving. Vera had been in Spain; she had escaped from a German prison camp. I admired her Marlene Dietrich bones and bold manner, and knew that in France she had been married to Peter Suvchinsky, one of the founders of the Eurasian movement, and so a close friend of Tsvetaeva's husband, Sergei Efron.

It was this last which brought me to visit her for the first time in the Cambridge hospital where she had been taken after a fall.

'I hope you haven't brought *flowers*,' she greeted me without preamble. 'What I need is a bottle of good red wine.'

Fortunately, I had been alerted this was the case, and poured red wine into a cup which should have held Ribena. After her first mouthfuls, she was eager to tell me about an encounter with T.S. Eliot some twenty years earlier. He had agreed to see her, but they had not hit it off. Somehow she managed to convert that snub into a criticism of Eliot's prudery. I was impatient. I wanted her to talk about Tsvetaeva, but she seemed reluctant to do so and even when she began I could hear that, although she admired Tsvetaeva's poetry, she did not like the woman. She chose to condemn her slovenliness but I guessed what she found most offensive was an arrogance founded on talent rather than beauty. Of Sergei, however, she spoke warmly.

'He was handsome, genial, friendly,' she said. '*Of course* I liked him more than her. When I was in hospital, having a child with great difficulty – I had to lie with my legs up in the air so as not to lose it – he came to see me every day.'

She deplored his fidelity to Tsvetaeva: 'There *was* another woman, you know. She was Swiss, and her father a millionaire. Sergei could have gone off with her, but he refused. He decided she was not the right one for him and stayed in Meudon with Marina. And do you know the reason he gave? He said he couldn't leave such an important poet.'

Over the years Vera told me many stories, in her low, cigarette-husky voice. To some I listened with polite incredulity. Most have since turned out to be true. One day, when she was entertaining me in her shabby bedsitter on the far side of Jesus Green, she described her return to Russia in 1937, the year the Russians call the *Yezhovchina*, when Yezhov, then boss of the NKVD, organised the most murderous of Stalin's great purges. When she visited Yezhov, he stood up without preamble to warn her in agitation: 'Go now. See no one. Go straight to the airport and leave. If you stay here, I cannot protect you.'

She obeyed, and reached Paris safely. I failed to ask what she was doing, calling on Yezhov in the first place. I know now that she had gone to plead for the release of her lover, once a prince, then a dedicated Communist. It was with him she had returned to Russia two years earlier. His arrest and disappearance had been unexpected. I did not enquire what her relationship had been to Yezhov.

Her beauty had brought her little happiness. She had been married three times, but when I knew her she was alone. And poor, though sometimes she had grand visitors. Solzhenitzyn, for instance, came to see her when he was writing *August 1914*. He wanted to investigate the memories she had of her father's study. She was more interested in the waifs and strays, for whom she always had house room. A handsome young layabout slept on her floor for six months. When I asked her why she allowed herself to be ripped off so blatantly, she shrugged and told me she was bored.

'You know, I think I was only happy for three months out of my whole life and the only thing that makes my living bearable now is knowing I can always end it.'

I have never felt like that, even in the wasteland of widowhood. There was something a little puritanical, however, in my insistence on activity. Why else would I have arranged to meet Daniel?

Daniel was the son of an old Cambridge friend, working for a year as a professor at the University of St Petersburg, and he collected me one evening to take me out to supper. I barely recognised him. He was pale, with fair hair, but now there was a stubble of darker beard pushing up through his skin, and when he spoke he kept his voice low; it was hard to catch his words. He seemed to be strung too tight, as if under some intolerable strain. I recognised something of myself in him.

'What are you doing here this time?' he asked.

'Working,' I said shortly.

Once on the street, Daniel put up his hand to hail a passing car, though the restaurant was not far away. It is a commonplace, inexpensive way to get round Russian cities.

I was already sorry I had agreed to meet him. He was a distinguished economist, who understood the New Russia far better than I did, but we had little in common. We stood at the kerbside, in the freezing sleet, and perhaps to amuse himself, he began to tease me. He believed material prosperity would transform the Russian spirit, and mocked my attachment to the literature of the past century. Indeed, even as he thanked me for sending him a copy of my recent biography, he could not resist adding, 'People here say your Akhmatova is the other face of Stalin.' I rose to the bait hotly even as we clambered into a green Volkswagen, and he replied with malicious glee: 'In Putin's Russia, print runs for poetry are no bigger than ours in the West, and this is how it should be: people love poetry as they love God, when life has nothing else to offer. And, in any case, these Russian writers you love so much, they all hated Jews.'

I knew he was right about the ancient Russian loathing of Jews, but found myself arguing: 'Anna Akhmatova and Marina Tsvetaeva took Jewish lovers, Marina's husband was a Jew. And where would Russian literature of the twentieth century be without Osip Mandelstam, Isaac Babel and Boris Pasternak?'

At this, the driver turned his head and observed in fluent English, 'She is right, you know.' He had a dark, Italianate face and brilliant eyes.

13

'There are many other drivers willing to take passengers,' Daniel observed uneasily.

Seeing his uncertainty, the driver swiftly offered a card neatly printed in roman script. He was an actor, at the moment unemployed.

'I remember now,' said Daniel suddenly. 'You played the devil Woland in the Taganka production of *The Master and Margarita*. Isn't that so?'

Our driver nodded and, as he turned to smile, I thought he truly resembled the Devil, with his glittering eyes and narrow face. I was a little troubled. If the Devil ever appeared in contemporary St Petersburg, he would surely have the same alarming confidence, and the citizens of this city would no doubt behave with the same greed as those of Bulgakov's Soviet Moscow.

'You see that police station?' our driver remarked. 'That is where Raskolnikov confessed his crimes to the Inspector.'

Ghosts everywhere, I thought. A city of ghosts. Even the characters in a novel have an afterlife here.

The restaurant was out of the tourist way, and not particularly grand, but to my irritation I had to let Daniel pay for the meal, since I discovered I had no money. I don't know where my wallet was stolen from me. I may have been robbed in the few moments taking shelter from the rain in a coffee shop near the Hermitage where I talked to a couple of friendly Tazhiks. As if to confirm his control of the situation, Daniel changed my English cheque for £200.

As I lay in bed that night – suddenly far too hot since the heating had come on and water was boiling in the radiators – I knew I had to report the loss at a police station because my insurance required it. The police would be wearily indifferent but they would give me a piece of paper. As I dropped into sleep, I wondered whether I would meet some image of Dostoevsky's Inspector Porfiry, and if he would be an old KGB apparatchik.

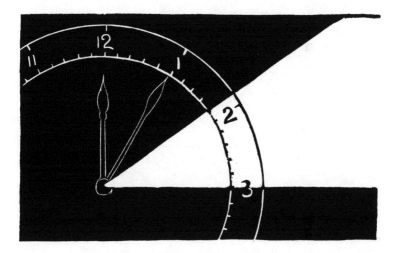

3 The Underworld Opens

In Raskolnikov's police station a screen saver swirled on the iMac, but the desk was littered with heaps of paper, wire trays, staplers and a Sellotape tin of cigarette butts. The man behind the desk was not dressed as a policeman. He wore a blue trilby hat, slanted to a thirties gangster angle, and his thick neck protruded from an open shirt.

'Passport. Tickets. Visa,' he said.

I gave him my documents and told my story.

He did not hand over the Form of Complaint I expected. He seemed to have something quite else on his mind as he stared at me.

'Your business in St Petersburg?'

'A tourist,' I said.

'It says here WRITER. What do you write?'

I hesitated.

'Poems, mainly.'

'So you like Russian poetry?'

'Of course.'

'Then perhaps I can interest you. Follow me.'

I was intrigued, if puzzled, and obeyed him.

'Forget Putin's Russia,' he said. 'The pastries with cloud-berry jam in the Astoria Hotel. The oligarchs, the store windows of sable coats, the caviar, the tourist tat. Put Nevsky Prospekt out of your mind. We are going back through the many names of the city, each one with its own ghosts. Are you ready? I want to show you my city. Not the Rastrelli staircases, the palaces, the golden domes, but the shabby rooms where I learnt to love poetry. Don't be surprised. In Russia even policemen love poetry.'

'Who are these people? With heavy overcoats?'

'The hoods and pimps of the inner city. Now they are Mafia, then they were KGB. To go back is like opening a wooden doll. Look around you. The advertisements for Big Macs and Coca-Cola are fading. There on the wall is Lenin wearing his worker's cap with a carnation in his lapel. Now we are in brilliant sunlight on the quay beside the *Aurora*.'

'To hear the shot that fired the Revolution?'

'Please don't be foolish. Look at the clothes.'

'Then what is the euphoria in the streets?'

'A coup has been defeated. People on the pavements are trying to sell carrots and bunches of herbs, and a brass band of youngsters is playing *Deutschland über alles*.'

'I can hear that, but why?'

'This is the day Leningrad took back its old name of St Petersburg. For these children, Germans are only tourists.'

'Don't they know about the siege?'

'For them, that is all grandmothers' tales. Hold on. We are going back through the seasons. Now it is hot summer, with the asphalt melting. The shops are empty. Look at the faces of those who come to buy.'

'Their faces are closed to me.'

'These are Soviet times. We must go further back.'

'I can't go so quickly; it's slippery. And the cinder smoke makes my eyes water.'

'It is a harsh year. Follow this crooked street.'

My companion now removed his hat, and I could see that his hair was white, and far longer than I imagined. My trust in him began to fade. Above me, I could make out nothing of the way I had come. I felt like a potholer who has climbed too far down and fears it may be impossible to return to the surface.

'Here you are,' he said.

I stared around me. Was this the Underworld? A steamy cloud which smelt of hot irons on damp cloth like an old-fashioned laundry? There were twittering sounds, like birds. Or the sound of grasshoppers rubbing their legs together. It was the sound made by human shadows: a crowd of them pressed towards me, blindly, their flesh seemingly as flimsy as that of moths.

I guessed at their faces. A young man with large melancholy eyes resembled a camel. A woman with the delicate features of a doll. By the minute, their bodies became more substantial, their gestures firmer. A slight, narrow-shouldered figure with his head thrown back detached itself from the others. From a mutter of conversation, one line suddenly sang out above the others: *We shall meet again in St Petersburg, as if we had buried the sun there.*

As the mist began to disperse, I made out streetcars and a flower shop. It was a winter afternoon, with yellow sky, and lamps already glittering in the shop windows.

4 The Stray Dog

This is St Petersburg, 1913: a glitter
of candles like icicles. On the streets,
a darkness after the theatre.

I am floating down the steps of The Stray Dog
into an airless cellar with a brass chandelier,
below the cobbles of Mikhailovskoye Square.

The light flickers and the rooms
are filled with wine and tobacco fumes.
Everything is permitted to poets here.

Outside there are drifts of snow. The sea wind's rage,
driving a few clouds wildly over the moon
– a silver moon lighting the Silver Age.

And nobody wonders at my living breath.
I am invisible, and in any case these people
give little thought to death.

They are frivolous because they don't yet know
this is the last year of their old world. *But
their horoscopes were all cast long ago.*

At a side table sits Anna Akhmatova
fingering a necklace of black agate,
equally bored by some desolate admirer

and her own husband, sprawling close to his mistress.
She is waiting for a scraggy boy, with long eyelashes,
to begin reading. After his words,

she imagines a swan gliding past river birds.
Silence. Time pauses. When it runs again,
these people, feasting on wine and roses

– as in Pushkin's time of plague – have become shadows.
This is Mandelstam's Petropolis;
a city dying like a ruined star.

And who approaches me in a shabby dress,
stepping like a mountain goat through the rubble?
A boyish figure, with a loose limbed gait.

So I call out: 'Marina Ivanovna,
I have no foothold in this desperate country.
Be my guide, although you never knew me.'

5 The River Station, Moscow 1941

I am no longer in St Petersburg. Nor in the Silver Age. This is a station waiting room, with people huddled on the floor, leaning against suitcases. Several are young soldiers. Others have faces I recognise; an old friend, for instance, with his child's underlip puffing as he talked. And there, sitting on a bench, is a woman who resembles Marina Tsvetaeva in middle age. She looks weary, as she had standing on the cobbles of Clamart one day in 1933, staring towards her chubby son, an old cardigan tucked into a black skirt. Her life has already happened to her, making her gaunt, etching two lines from her nose to her mouth. Her hair is cropped short and her eyes barely focus. She holds a cigarette which has burned down to her fingers.

People are looking at her curiously, with a certain hostility. Her sleeves are secured with a safety pin. There are holes in her skirt. Yet her clothes, though shabby, are not Soviet and she is wearing strings of amber.

She is unaware of their gaze. Or the flies. Her eyes are yellowish, like those of a jungle animal.

Her face changes with her thoughts. There are no bones to preserve composure. She is lighting one cigarette from another. She rolls them with her own fingers, dragging the acrid, home-grown tobacco smoke into her lungs. The past is irrevocable. She would like to shake it out of her head. Burning ash covers her skirt.

Her mind is bloodless, starved of nourishment. Trails of thought cross the emptiness. Fragments of another world. A beach in the Crimea. A meek young boy of seventeen with eyes too large for his face, looking for a cornelian in the sand. He is Sergei Efron, Seryozha, from a family of revolutionaries. That he has Jewish blood pleases her. All her heroes have always been outlaws and heretics.

He is the first man to enter her bed. And he is clumsy, but she doesn't care, because she loves him. Once they are together they are happy, as children are happy. Even now, with everything lost, she remembers. They will marry. They will have to marry because their first encounters leave her pregnant.

Here at the river station crowds of peasants, *kholkhozniks*, and a few men in uniform are waiting for a steamer to take them north on the River Volga. The war has begun, and the Germans are sweeping into Russia. They are still far from Moscow but some bombardment can be heard at a distance. If Tsvetaeva hears, she gives no sign.

Near the ramp leading to the boats, a girl of three or four begins to cry. Snot runs from her nose. She is pale and probably feverish. Her mother gives a glancing blow to the side of the child's head and the wild crying dwindles into sobs.

It was like the blow of a friendly bear. Animal. No cruelty in it, Tsvetaeva observes without rancour, remembering her own mother; that narrow passionate woman who had driven her to excel so harshly. With words. Contempt. The only reality in her childhood was her mother's ferocity. For a moment, Tsvetaeva remembers the high ceilings, parquet floors and potted plants of the House on Three Ponds Lane and can hear Chopin played on the grand piano. Another world. And an unhappy one, she remembers, thinking of those endless music lessons she endured, the way she was refused writing paper. The loneliness between her parents. And her mother's last words: 'I only regret music and the sun.'

Her own gifted daughter, Alya, became her playmate, her accomplice, her nurse; a loving acolyte, a poet, an artist. There were whispers in the houses of rich friends about the way she exploited her. Alya was willing. Too willing. Until, suddenly … but Marina cannot bear to remember the first sullen rebellion. The shift in domestic loyalty. Marina ponders her own selfishness in putting poetry before every other duty. A wickedness like the sin of her imagined Marusya, who loved her Vampire so much she fed her whole family to him. Now Alya is in a labour camp. Her thoughts recoil from that pain.

Not that she had any illusions that she would find happiness in her homeland when she returned from France. She followed Seryozha out of Russia, when he escaped to the West after the Civil War. She followed him back when he had to run away from France as a spy. She remembers writing: *If God performs this miracle and leaves you alive, I will follow you like a dog.* Twenty-one years later, in Vanves, she wrote, bitterly: *And go I shall, like a dog.*

After so many years in exile, she no longer recognises her native city. Everything in it has changed too much. The poplars around her childhood house are long gone. When she runs to one-time friends, begging help, most are reluctant to see her. Ilya Ehrenburg at least meets her, but his eyes are hooded and blank, his mind filled with other disasters. Ehrenburg – Ehrenburg, who had given up his own attic so that she and Alya had somewhere to stay in Berlin, who brought her the first letter from Boris Pasternak – Ehrenburg hardly registers her presence. All his attention is swallowed by the German threat.

Strangers. She has so often been a stranger. In Prague where her slatternly ways were despised by the house-proud émigrés, or in Paris where her poverty made her a beggar to rich friends. For all the hardship, she survived through her poetry. Now once again in Moscow, her own city, she knows herself unwelcome. Dangerous, too, because her husband is in prison, and her daughter in the Gulag, and people are afraid to be with her. All she needed once was a bedside lamp, a notebook and a little silence. She could enter a world of dreams and fairy tales and write as if under a spell. Now she has not written a poem for nearly two years.

It is no longer clear why it is worth staying alive.

Suddenly there is a little rustle among those waiting for the boat. They have recognised someone notable, and they part to let him pass. Tsvetaeva turns to see Boris Pasternak coming towards her. The crowds give way respectfully. They know his handsome face. It is unmistakeable. Many of them know his poems. She lowers her own head as he comes up to press her hand. A quick goodbye? What else? He does not invite her to join him in his dacha at Peredelkino. Even to come was brave, she knows that but, when he leaves, her face is disappointed.

Loneliness.

She was most lonely in the dacha in Bolshevo which was Seryozha's reward for service to the State. Once unimaginable. Now acknowledged freely. A pleasant Moscow suburb. Her daughter Alya was there, happy with her new man, Mulya. There was a married couple, recruited by Efron in France. But she was alone, surrounded by believers in the new Soviet order. All of them reporting back to the NKVD. Everyone a willing spy, even Alya and Seryozha.

Until they took Alya and one of her friends for interrogation. Then Seryozha was taken, on Alya's testimony. Her mind draws back from that memory, but the pain of it colours her thoughts. Further back. Farther back.

She remembers the Civil War famine long ago, bartering for pig fat and millet in the countryside. She wasn't brought up to trade. She bought a wooden doll she didn't want and only succeeded in giving away three boxes of matches. The Red Army was everywhere. They ripped open featherbeds for jewellery. Back in Moscow, she and Alya dragged a sledge over the snow to return used bottles for a few kopecks. They left Irina tied to a chair for her own safety. She was too young to understand, and little children get used to anything. Tsvetaeva has tried for a quarter of a century to forget her pretty voice singing, 'Maeena, my Maeena'. And that when put in an orphanage, Irina died of starvation.

All her sexual passions failed miserably and, if she thinks of them, it is fleetingly. There was the poet Sofia Parnok, with her Jewish face as handsome as Beethoven. Marina once showered her with bracelets and gold chains, but that was long ago. She had never known such physical pleasure as she found under Parnok's fingers. But in Paris she heard of her death without much emotion. And when she was told, on this return to Moscow, that Parnok forgave and blessed her as she lay dying, she felt nothing. And what of dapper Konstantin Rodzevich who abandoned her for an ordinary woman and drew her greatest poetry from her in Prague? Under his hands her body arched with pleasure, but to be loved in return was something of which she had not mastered the art.

Another memory flickers into life. Seryozha in a tilted trilby hat, his underlip heavy as Ehrenburg's or Mandelstam's – two other Jews, after all – but not so slack. Green eyes under bushy eyebrows. The lines cut deep in his cheeks, like a Hollywood cowboy. A handsome man, working as a film extra.

The light has not yet gone, but the raids on the outskirts have already begun. The only windows are covered with strips of Sellotape to keep glass from flying when they shatter. She sees the pathetic barrage balloons in the sky. The Germans will take Moscow, as they took Prague and Paris, she says. They are her first words aloud, matter of fact, without resonance. No one answers her.

She does not say: *My husband is in prison. My daughter is in a labour camp. I don't know what's happening to them.*

Or: *I have spent the last two years looking for a hook.*

Even as I experience her desolate thoughts, I am aware of my own separate body. Unseen. Solid. Still breathing. Dressed in the clothes of a more comfortable era. I am suddenly ashamed of my old claim to resemble her. Her situation has always been so much more extreme than mine. All we had in common were desperation, a wild eccentricity, the long marriage, a sick husband, both of us working like a horse between the shafts to keep the family going. People found the stench of her flat repellent, especially the layers of grease in the kitchen. I had less excuse for my own disorder. Now she was a lost creature. Did I dare approach? She had been my Virgil, into the Russian twentieth century.

'Marina Ivanovna?' I begin, sitting next to her on the hard floor. It is late afternoon, but Moscow in August is hot, and there is little oxygen in the crowded room.

She peers at me, as if puzzled. There is no reason she should know me.

'Are you taking the boat to the River Kama?' she asks,

26

as if we were both ageing peasant women, between whom a moment of friendship was possible.

But she is staring at me as she fingers her amber necklace, as if I were some gypsy woman met on the muddy roads near Prague, as if I knew more than she did and could foretell her future. I remember how deeply superstitious she had always been, how any hint of foreknowledge would be bound to disturb her.

Now she asks my name, and nods when I give it to her, as if it confirms her opinion.

'Jewish, I suppose.'

'Yes,' I reply, stung by the ease with which she has identified me, and remembering her description of down-at-heel Jewish women like herrings, who shared her clerical job in the Moscow famine.

For the first time she looks friendly, even amused.

A plump sixteen-year-old boy comes towards her then to complain of thirst. I can see there is some animosity between them but she reaches into the sack she is carrying and brings out a bottle of water. He takes it ungraciously, and when he has drunk his fill gives it back to her, puts his hands deep into his pockets and leaves without another word. If he sees me, he makes no sign. It is her son Georgy, I realise, studying his handsome, selfish face. She watches him leave with an expression of pained tenderness.

'Georgy did not want to leave Moscow,' she says.

But she speaks less to me than to herself.

'He has fallen in love. He goes fire-watching with the girl on the top of our flats. He calls me an old crow. It doesn't matter. I want him to live. He is just sixteen. A brilliant boy. He deserves to live.'

'Where are you travelling?' I ask her, as if I knew nothing of her story.

'Towards Yelabuga. On the Kama.'

'Don't go,' I cry involuntarily, knowing she would take her own life there, that her body would hang from a nail in a peasant's hut.

At this, she draws back from me and once again there is an expression of distrust.

'An agent of the NKVD, then?' she murmurs, but after a few moments she shrugs as if nothing that could happen to her had much significance.

'No other way now. My life is over. Has been over for years. Listen. Marriage and love destroy. An early marriage like mine was a catastrophe. I suppose you know: my husband is in gaol. My daughter is in the Gulag. I have written nothing for two years. What else can you need to find out, whoever you are?'

'There are people you love.'

'*Do* you still love people?' she asks. 'I long ago stopped loving anything but animals and trees.'

Again, she looks intensely at me, her green myopic eyes puzzled. I long to explain my presence in her terrible life. To explain how her poems have given me courage from the moment I began to write. But I cannot find the words. And the river station is melting. Already people have begun to shimmer like figures in a mirage and I am losing their outlines. Yet I can hear her voice as if from beyond her own death. And her voice remains with me.

'If you come to Moscow in a different age, I will look after you.'

There is a sudden bustle, the doors open and an irritable crowd pushes its way toward the boat at the dockside.

6 Rivers

Rivers, we dream of black rivers, and
a shadowy world lying across their waters.
The other shore is always a little uncertain.

Darkness. Acacia blossom. No boatman.
I am not brave enough for this exploration.
This is a savage path. I fear this country.

where so many of my kin already lie
in unmarked graves, or have been thrown
without pity into ravines as hair and bone.

My guide is a gaunt, sure-footed spectre
who walks fearlessly into the night
murmuring, *'The Neva is not my river*

I cannot love St Petersburg. Once,
with a blizzard outside and a war raging,
I made a gypsy visit to the city

but I am from Moscow, the city Peter rejected,
where the domes burn and bells call us to prayer.
Only there can I be happy when I am dead.'

She beckons me past the Old Post Office
and a tower whose spire is drenched
by the full moon: her face is

solemn and her hair disordered.
We are walking. Walking. By a brown river
with a few ice floes. I follow her

until the yellow lights begin to flare
in window after window. And she tells me,
'This is the spring of 1934, when I was

in Paris by the railway line dreaming
of Prague. This is Stalin's Moscow,
and here are two of your extended family.'

7 Moscow 1934

It is almost Spring, a little slushy underfoot, ice floes still moving over the brown river, a glinting bright sun on the streets.

Two men walk towards me, one in a flat cap, stocky with thick glasses; he is square, like a Pole or a North German, with a thick bull neck. The other is sardonic, lanky of leg with a thin face, a cigarette sticking to his full under lip, and heavy lidded eyes. He looks French or perhaps Italian; he smells of Gitanes. Both would instantly be recognisable to a Russian as figures of Jewish life. They talk with animation: Isaac Babel, the most Jewish, the most Russian of writers. And Ilya Ehrenburg, the cleverest of cosmopolitans.

'Will these trees ever make it into spring?' Babel is grumbling. 'In the south there will be chestnuts in full flower by now, poplar fluff everywhere. And in Paris too, I imagine. What brings you here, Ilya? You love Paris. The old streets, the accordions …'

'Stalin's command.'

'A bad joke, my friend. But I forgive you. Will you come home for a meal? We shall have dumplings with sweet apricots. Come on. My wife thinks you don't like her. She is beautiful, supremely intelligent, and not in the least literary, which for me is a plus. An engineer. But I think you feel loyal to my first wife in Paris.'

'A little sorry for her.'

'She left me when I took up with another woman years ago. And when that went wrong, and I went to Paris to persuade her to give our lives together another shot –'

'I know. She would not return to Russia.'

'Well, I can't live in Paris, Ilya, not even to see my daughter grow up.'

'Heine spent twenty-five years in exile.'

'Listen. Heine was celebrated as a wit in Paris. I should be a taxi driver. Is it true that Stalin summoned you back to Russia?'

'So the Ambassador told me in Paris. Our French friends thought it a good sign. That Stalin is becoming more liberal.'

'You should have stayed in France. They believe anything there. Even the latest confessions. What do you care? You were never a Communist.'

'I care because the friendship of Western democracies is shit. And there is the little matter of Adolf Hitler.'

'You were in Spain?'

'I was. Isaac, they say you meet Stalin often at Gorky's dacha.'

'Legends, Ilya. They also say he wanted me to write a novel about him.' Babel's eyes crinkle up mischievously. 'Would that be a sensible ambition? At the moment, all I want is to warm myself in a little Odessa sunshine. I don't need elegant furniture. I can write on a kitchen table.'

'What are you writing now?'

'Not much.'

'Are there problems with censorship?'

'I censor myself. Two lines out here, a phrase or two there...'

'No more stories?'

'In any self-respecting capitalist country, I would have long since died of starvation.'

'You have stopped writing altogether?'

'No. I write scripts. With Eisenstein. Sometimes they are even made into films.'

'The whole world would be excited to see them.'

'You speak for the world, let me speak for Moscow. What I like most these days is to potter in junk shops with bits and pieces for sale. Second-hand slippers, a stuffed eagle. There is no room for them in my flat, sadly.'

'You were always a collector.'

'Be very careful how you write about your past, Ilya. But I am teaching my grandmother to suck eggs. You know the whole scene by instinct, even without living here. Yesterday a woman came to see me. Her husband is in trouble. He is not an enemy of the people, she says, so why does he confess to such crimes? He has done nothing wrong. I explain: everyone has to confess. It's their Soviet duty.'

'Isaac, I shall leave for Paris tomorrow. Can I do anything for you?'

'How is it you come and go as you like? You must have the ear of the great.'

'No. I have the ear of Paris, where a great many intellectuals admire our Soviet way of life. So I have my uses.'

'Hmm.'

'Some things don't play so well over there. That's all.'

As the two men pass us, they look sideways, perhaps out of habit, perhaps sensing our presence, perhaps suddenly made cautious as they approach the yellow stucco building of the Rostov house. Ehrenburg pauses to relight his pipe.

Outside the house there are police who are sorting out a quarrel between two drunken men.

'Who knows what that is about,' Ilya shrugs.

'Look at that magnificent woman. Over there. A Georgian, would you say? Or perhaps Azerbaijani. That is what it is about. It is not political. We love large women in Moscow.'

'Fat women?'

'The fatter the better. So. I wish you much merriment, Ilya. There is nothing finer. And good food. On Gogol Street in Odessa there is a bakery where you can buy bagels with poppy seeds. You know Solomon Mikhoels?'

Ehrenburg is startled.

'He is well, I hope?'

'He can't forget his first wife. He goes into the closet and kisses her clothes. You see how intensely we make relationships? Tell my daughter she is a princess. With a run-down king for a father.'

They pass, and their voices can no longer be heard. Babel, the thicker set of the two, looks indestructible. Ehrenburg, with his cough and lack of muscle, looks altogether weaker.

But he will survive.

8 Ilya Ehrenburg in Gehinnom

He turns, a cigarette holder between slender
    fingers, as if still in his
Paris of singers and zinc counters,
    his eyelids half-closed,

his face amused. He and Marina move
    to embrace each other, over ice
green as bottle glass, the wind blowing
    street grit and cinders.

She knows his praise preserved her poems,
    and not without danger;
he honours her ferocious genius.
    As for the slurs –

of wily self-serving, black complicity –
    his tribe is well-rehearsed;
they have endured
    nine hundred captivities;

he has always known he belonged to those
    Russia thought it prudent
to chastise, even before conspirators.
    Jews are the canaries in the mine.

9 Moscow, December 1937

Ehrenburg and his wife Lyubova are leaving for Moscow by train, taking a roundabout route to avoid Nazi Germany. They are both in low spirits. He has seen dead children and exhausted old women in the streets of Barcelona, and fears the war in Spain has moved decisively against the Republicans. He is disgusted by French cowardice and treachery. There are constant rumours of war with Hitler. Strikes. Confrontations between Right and Left.

Ehrenburg is the most famous Russian journalist in the West. He has been at the centre of the emigration in Berlin, Paris and Madrid since his days in Montparnasse before the First World War. His wit, charm and command of French has made it easy for him to make friends with notable figures in the arts, including Picasso and André Malraux. No longer a Bolshevik, he remains a furious opponent of Fascism, and thinks the Soviet Union the only force capable of standing up to Hitler.

He had been told many times that when Soviet diplomats or journalists are called back to Russia, they often disappear. In Spain there were rumours of widespread purges and assassinations. People who whispered of them were often convinced Bolsheviks. Even though he had seen the Cheka at work in Kiev in the Civil War, Ehrenburg always dismissed these stories as exaggerations and more or less believed what he said. Rulers only did what was useful to keep themselves in power. What advantage could there be in such indiscriminate butchery?

36

He intends to make a very short trip to Moscow. He has taken Lyubova with him, in the hope that her jealousy will be assuaged in his company. He has never promised fidelity and never deceived her, but he knows she is afraid of being abandoned. He is the only centre of her life. A talented painter, she has never pursued her work with much energy. She even developed a nervous disorder in the muscles of her legs after his affair with the beautiful Denise LeCache.

He has no great fear about returning to the Soviet Union for himself. His reports for *Izvestia* were not much censored and, rather as he had on the front line, walking between shells, he feels safe enough. This time, however, he does not know what he is walking into. It is December 1937. The year of the Great Terror.

He plans to stay with his daughter Irina, the child of an early passionate love affair with Yekaterina Schmidt. Irina is his only child, but he is content to have her stay in the Soviet Union. He is not possessive. She lives with her husband Boris Lapin in the Writers' House in Lavrushinsky Lane. Pasternak lives in the same ten-storey building.

He and Lyubova are exhausted when they arrive. The streets are deep in snow and a wind is getting up which drives icy flurries into their faces. It is minus 20 degrees and even with their ear flaps down and tied under the chin, the cold bites into their flesh. And although Irina and Boris help to bring their baggage into the house like dutiful children, Ehrenburg detects some anxiety in their welcome.

He observes that Irina looks morose, even sullen, almost as if she were angry with him for returning. The strangeness is palpable. Even going up in the lift there are signs of it. A notice forbids the flushing of books down the latrines and threatens tenants who do so.

Ehrenburg points to it and asks, 'Is it a joke?'

His daughter is furious with him, touches her finger to her lips.

'You really know nothing then?'

He stares at her and shrugs. Lyubova looks frightened.

'Why did you come back?' Irina demands.

He has no answer for her, but helps Lyubova out of the lift, feeling physically weak himself.

In the flat, he asks about old friends. The news is black.

'How is Boris Pilnyak?'

'Taken.'

'But why?'

'How should I know why? Nobody knows.'

'In prison then?'

Ehrenburg has been in prison, as a schoolboy revolutionary, in a Tsarist gaol. They beat him and broke his teeth. But what he remembers is the loneliness of it, how the sounds of an early morning streetcar made him sick for home. He read Chekhov. Perhaps Gorky, or was that later? His father bribed someone and he was released. Some of this he tells his daughter.

'Times have changed,' she says sternly. 'They let you have books in gaol then?'

'Yes.'

Her laugh is scornful and bitter. For a while, he tries to get under the black curtain of resentment with jokes, but nothing amuses her. He becomes serious.

'Don't writers speak up for Pilnyak?'

'Nobody would dare,' she tells him.

Lapin listens to this interchange uneasily. He is a talented writer, and a courageous explorer of remoter parts of the Soviet Union. Ehrenburg approves of him as a husband for his daughter. Now Lapin interrupts Ehrenburg brusquely, advising him.

'Please don't ask anyone else these questions. And if someone raises such matters, just keep quiet.'

Now Ehrenburg listens to the lift going up and down in the Writers' House on Lavrushinsky, and every time the lift stops, with a jerk, he looks up. He understands. No one else is asleep either. The whole house of flats is listening. They are wondering when the next arrest will come, and who it will be. One day perhaps there will be a knock for him. He keeps a case packed with two changes of underwear.

One night, while he is walking his dog, unable to sleep, Ehrenburg meets Pasternak with a dog of his own. They walk through the snowdrifts together in a shared, troubled silence, until Pasternak begins to wave his hands and mutters, 'If only someone would tell Stalin what is happening.'

It was common in those days for people to comfort themselves with the thought that Stalin knew nothing of what was happening to the intelligentsia.

Ehrenburg's plan had been to return to Spain in two weeks, but when he asks for an exit visa his request is unexpectedly refused.

'Things take time, now, Ilya,' he was told. 'You have to be patient.'

'But I am needed.'

'We know about your work in Spain.'

'It's not just a question of Spain. Talented writers in the West must join the fight against Fascism. Stalin appointed me to that fight. I should be there.'

No one is impressed by the argument.

39

The weeks tick by. His daughter's tension becomes even more visible. He guesses unhappily that his presence makes her own position dangerous. He longs to see Babel, the 'wise rabbi' as he thinks of him, but he is said to be in Yalta for his asthma. Ehrenburg hopes it is true.

'My life has come to resemble vaudeville,' he tells Lyubova.

'You have always lived like a chameleon,' she replies, not altogether affectionately.

In January, his daughter tells him that Vsevelod Meyerhold has lost his theatre. Ehrenburg is thrown onto the defensive, as if personally responsible.

'I have always defended his genius. I saw his triumph in Paris. Everyone admired him. From Picasso to René Clair.'

Worse is to come. Stalin arranges for Ehrenburg to be given a pass for the trial of his old friend and patron Nikolai Bukharin, once editor of *Izvestia*, who, with twenty other defendants, is accused of forming a cell led from abroad by Leon Trotsky. There is no outcry, although Bukharin had been not only a good friend to Ehrenburg but also an honest supporter of many writers in trouble.

In court, Ehrenburg can barely recognise his once handsome friend. The thin, broken man in the dock is little more than a shadow. In a low monotone, he confesses to monstrous crimes, sealing his own fate. Ehrenburg can barely speak when he returns to Lavrushinsky Lane. He lies down on the sofa with his face to the wall and refuses all food.

On 15 March, after Bukharin's execution, Ehrenburg writes directly to Stalin, begging permission to return to Spain. It may be that the letter never reached Stalin.

Ehrenburg is simply told that his request has been denied, and he is advised to have his books and belongings brought from Paris.

Trapped.

He reflects that he had often been close to death. In Spain his car had collided with a truck carrying artillery shells. He has always lived on his wits and his pen. Rashly, and against the objections of Irina and Lyubova, who fear such an impudence can only bring about his arrest, Ehrenburg writes a second letter to Stalin. He has no great hope that the risk will pay off. For weeks they hear nothing. He listens to the elevator stop and start, quarrels with his daughter.

Waits.

Then, inexplicably, Stalin responds with permission.

A few days after May Day 1938, he and Lyubova are allowed to leave by train for Helsinki. Once in Finland, they sit on a bench in a public garden, unable to talk to one another, bewildered by their own escape. For a time.

10 Pasternak on the cinder slopes

Under yellow street lights, one blurry outline
sharpens into the lumbering figure
of Boris Pasternak, his face
at once an Arab and his horse.
  My guide turns back.

'Cowardice, cowardice,' she mutters.
'So many of this poet's words sustained me
though we only touched in letters.
We could have met in Weimar. Or Berlin.
  We might have visited a living Rilke.

Yet, even as he called me heaven
and wife, I knew I never counted
in the masculine present; and I did not want
to discover he could not find Eve
  in me, but Psyche.

In Paris? No. *That was a non-meeting.*
He was tongue-tied, uneasy,
sick, too frightened to answer
anyone directly. We were no more
  than edgy strangers.

Walk here. The air is clearer. Follow the scent
of the earth flowering in a late spring.
For him, raindrops were heavy as cufflinks,
wet lilac like a sparrow in a rainstorm.
  Our only shared passion was poetry.'

11 Peredelkino 1937

Half an hour out of Moscow is the writers' village of Peredelkino.

It is a warm afternoon. And there he is. Hatless and shirtless in a garden, drinking with two guests. He has a broad face, huge eyes and his cheekbones have deep hollows beneath them.

There are banks of flowers. A lilac bush. Lavender. The poet looks calm and happy. He has been digging a dark patch of earth under the fruit trees, and the spade still stands in the soil. He is wearing old clothes, and the lowest button on the right side of his jacket hangs by a thread. He moves a deckchair into the shade for one of his guests.

This woman, I observe with astonishment, is my old friend Vera Traill. When I knew her in Cambridge, late in her life, she was still beautiful. Now she resembles a star of silent films. Accepting the chair, she leans towards the poet and begins to talk with animation about her work in Moscow on the translation of children's books. Pasternak has been translating Georgian poets, and nods agreeably as if talking to an equal. She seems comfortable in the conversation, as if unaware of Pasternak's greatness.

The man standing at her side is bald and bearded and bears a fleeting resemblance to Lenin, in spite of yellow, misplaced teeth and horn-rimmed spectacles. He is uneasy and at the same time, as he looks at Vera, plainly one who adores.

Tsvetaeva hisses at me: *'That man has the soul of a stuffed capon. When he sees apple trees in blossom he is reminded of cauliflower in a white sauce.'*

The level of her hostility surprises me, and offers me a clue to the man's identity. This must be Dmitri Svyatopolk Mirsky, the famous literary critic, Vera's lover. Once a prince, now a fanatic Marxist, he is in Moscow to be part of the new Soviet experiment. Vera has joined him, though she refuses to marry him.

Some years earlier, Tsvetaeva spent three weeks with Mirsky in London. Their one night together had gone badly; their days too. He wanted to visit museums, while she preferred markets and the great historic bridges. In several poems she chides him as a *gourmand*. He teases her equally for her indifference to *haute cuisine*: 'One may as well give you hay.'

As we watch, Pasternak's new wife, Zinaida Nikolaevna, brings out cold drinks. She does not have the languorous Jewish beauty of Pasternak's first wife Yevgenia, but some traces of an illicit honeymoon in Georgia with Pasternak still hang about her. And her brisk movements speak of household order and a peaceful life. Pasternak has had enough of Bohemia, and no wish for another artist in his family. Her background was Russian Orthodox. He liked that. But as she returns to the kitchen, I have the impression she is displeased with someone; perhaps Pasternak, perhaps Vera.

The garden is hot and sheltered, and the drinks are welcome. Mirsky, who has twice signalled his need to return to Moscow, postpones his departure. He perches awkwardly on a bench. The conversation turns to literature.

Mirsky speaks of James Joyce, and the uselessness of modernism. He praises Pasternak, however, as he has done recently and publicly and not without some danger to himself. When he takes his formal leave, Pasternak courteously invites Vera to remain: it will be hot in Moscow; the air in the countryside is fresher. Vera agrees without fuss. It had clearly been her intention to do so all along.

Tsvetaeva watches Pasternak and Vera with a certain bitterness. She is a woman of genius watching a beauty with no more than ordinary intelligence flirting easily with a great man. She longs to intervene, to speak directly to one of the few human beings she regards as her spiritual equal. But she cannot be seen or heard. So we listen and watch together.

At first, Pasternak is talking about Shakespeare. It is hard to make out his words, but his voice has a kindly, apologetic music in contrast to Vera's piercing assurance. He throws out his arms as he struggles to explain his admiration. 'You see, Shakespeare holds nothing in reserve, he spends himself completely...' Pasternak does not finish one sentence before some other thought presses to make itself felt. Then he loses the thread of what he is saying.

But Vera is on another tack in any case. She is asking about his childhood, his family in Odessa, his painter father. He describes what he remembers willingly, but in fragments. As he speaks, I imagine a candlelit room in Moscow, his mother at the piano, Tolstoy among the guests; the immense privilege of the intelligentsia in pre-Revolutionary Russia. The casual mix of Gentile and Jew. The common, humane assumptions.

It seems not to be the answer she wanted, however. He replies at a slant. It is not an inheritance he is proud of. He does not like to remember how many Jews were among the intelligentsia. He has never liked their irony; or their jokes, which always seemed to him a kind of whistling in the dark. He likes to say his nanny secretly baptised him as a child. It may be true. In any case, he treasures her peasant stories, her Russian superstitions. He cannot understand why any Jew would want to hold on to his own rituals. Why could they not dissolve among the rest of the Russian people? Such foolishness, to wear the kind of dress that made it possible to pick them out on sight, to huddle together so they could all be found and destroyed. He is sickened by the thought of a river in sunshine during the Civil War, and the pogroms that murdered so many in the villages nearby. A stubborn choice of martyrdom. *Why should so many clever, kind people* choose *to go on being mocked and slaughtered throughout the centuries?*

And his father? His mother? Odessa Jews both, though the household was altogether secular. His father had refused to convert, even when it might have been an advantage to do so. His mother was a child prodigy at the piano. Music filled her childhood. Even after her marriage, when she gave up her concert career, she had only to sit down on her red velvet chair and play to earn applause. Music was truly her religion.

He loves them deeply: Leonid, his handsome father whose genius as a painter of portraits had brought his son Tolstoy, and Rilke too, and given him a relish for everyday life, however much of his own he gave to art. Boris is proud of them both. They are figures of an eighteenth-century Enlightenment. They are now in Berlin, he reflects, where they have already been informed officially that they are non-Aryan.

He tells Vera where they are, and she is astonished.

'How can they stay in Germany?'

'Well, they may come and live with me. I have a new Moscow flat which is big enough for all of us. In

Lavrushinksy. But I think they will follow my sister, who has married an Englishman and lives in north Oxford.'

There were other possibilities which Pasternak does not mention. His father had taken a trip to Palestine in 1924, and been overcome by emotion as he looked about him at an alien landscape of black cypress trees and dazzling dusty roads. Some holy Jewish sepulchre had moved him. Pasternak knows his father attended Zionist meetings in Berlin, but puts the thought from his mind. 'On balance it seems likeliest he will go to England,' he repeats.

She nods. 'And Osip Mandelstam?'

He hesitates. 'He is in Voronezh with Nadezhda.'

Now he is watching her. He must have heard the rumours that she is a spy, but one in ten are spies and she is charming, so he continues to flirt with her, in his slow bumbling way that leaves women to make all the advances, as if he were a tree with sweet fruit, willing to allow any woman to pick what she wants from him.

'You have to know how to surrender to idleness. A line of poetry comes after hours of forcing yourself, and in that idleness suddenly… sometimes…' He stops. 'What have I done yet? Nothing. And now I translate. I shall never write anything comparable to Mandelstam's *Stone*.'

His face clouds. He does not usually go out of his way to praise Mandelstam, who is well known to be in trouble. But the preceding night he had been troubled by a guilty dream of him – unkempt, ill, unhappy – in his Voronezh exile, and woken grimly into the usual agony: the shock of Stalin's voice on the telephone in 1934, the first moment of incredulity, Stalin's question: Is Mandelstam a great poet? Then the chilling memory of his own hesitation before Stalin reproached him for not speaking up for his friend.

He is embarrassed to remember his own pretentious

lunacy, his suggestion that Stalin might want to discuss Life and Death. He can still hear the blank purr as Stalin put the phone down. Felt his own desperation as he tried to ring the Kremlin back and failed, naturally.

Pasternak had told the story many times, with many variations. Those with their own jealousies reported the incident as a sign of envy or cowardice. But Nadezhda never held it against him.

Of course Mandelstam was a genius. Only, Pasternak honestly did not approve of his poem about the Kremlin mountaineer. Mandelstam had spoken it to him, once, as they walked in the street. It was such a foolish lampoon. To write of Stalin's pock-marked skin. To accuse him of murdering peasants? It was a suicide note.

Into his mind came an ancient, tribal thought: *a Jew should know better.*

There were rumours that Mandelstam had gone mad in prison, that he had jumped out of a window and broken his arm and was having hallucinations about his wife in mountainous Cherdyn. Then he was brought back from the Urals. Akhmatova made the long journey to visit him in Voronezh, in the region of the Black Earth, and reported him still capable of gaiety. They read Dante together.

Vera had been talking, and he smiled, to disguise the long way his thoughts had wandered away from her. Then he said:

'Tell me. You are a friend of Marina Ivanovna and her husband. We met briefly in Paris, a year or so back. I worry …'

Vera's pencil-thin eyebrows rise as his sentence drifts away.

'I could not sleep in Paris. I would not have dared to visit her, but she came to find me at the Congress. Even in rags, she was still…' His voice trails off. 'We walked the streets together. But there are problems in the family. Disagreements. They are hideously poor. Her husband and daughter are planning a return to Russia. Both Communist, I believe. Marina was even considering the journey herself. I did not advise her as I should.' Then he mutters, 'Well, I was half-mad. I dared not let my parents even see my state.'

There was a chill in Vera's response: 'Tsvetaeva is a wonderful poet, of course. It was I who told Mirsky of her greatness.'

'He might have seen that for himself.' Pasternak's voice has a hint of reproach. 'She soared above all of us.'

He falls silent.

'However, as to politics,' Vera continues, 'she is like a child. She thought Kerensky was a Napoleon. Now she doesn't even read the papers.'

'I don't like to do so either,' Pasternak mutters. 'It kills the present moment to be always waiting for news of what is happening elsewhere.'

He does not speak of show trials. Of implausible confessions. Of what he knows that this young woman, not long arrived from France, seems not to know. For a moment, he considers telling her exactly what had driven him to seek refuge in a clinic a year earlier: his visit to the Ukraine. Images he cannot shake out of his head. The starving, frozen people; the families taken off in carts to Siberia without clothing or boots. The murderous famine.

He contents himself with describing his confusion, put on a train with Isaac Babel at the last moment to attend the

Congress in Paris. He wrote no speech. The audience applauded because they knew his name, and because he spoke of finding poetry in the ordinary world around them.

Vera yawned, and stretched as delicately as a cat. Lazily, and without particular emphasis, she asked, 'You are not a member of the Party yourself? Even though you support the Revolution?'

'I am a Communist. In the same sense as Peter the Great or Pushkin,' he assured her.

Then Zinaida appears with a shawl across her shoulders. She is walking to visit a friend and has left cold food for supper. For a moment, she sounds bad-tempered and a little bossy. Pasternak remains his usual genial self as he turns to Vera.

'Perhaps you would like to eat with me?'

Vera smiles at the invitation. She takes it as a tribute to her sexual allure, which is what she needs most from a man.

'I must leave, Boris. I have an appointment.'

'With whom?'

'Yezhov.'

His eyes close for a moment and when they open that willingness to be pillaged has left his face. He looks cautious. Yezhov is the lynchpin of Stalin's Great Terror. A dwarf. An evil man.

'You have dangerous friends,' he murmurs.

He looks unhappy, perhaps running their conversation through his mind to see if he has said anything worthy of report. It might be that his praise of Mandelstam was a little rash. Then, as if remembering the affection she had aroused, he adds: 'So be careful.'

In his apartment in Central Moscow, Mirsky sits at a table with a pile of books and a bottle of vodka. His hand is a little shaky, but he is not drunk. A month has passed. His curtains are open to the June night. He cannot sleep and cannot work. In the street below a Black Maria is already drawing up at his door.

12 Nashchokin Lane, Moscow

At night, in a sleepless city, Marina
is searching for Mandelstam, her beautiful brother,
looking in the snow for the very sledge
they once travelled in under a rug together,

past bell towers and cupolas. Nothing is lost
of the poems that belong to one another; she has
already given him Moscow with its rivers and churches,
saying: 'He will not repent that he once loved me,

my boy genius with long eyelashes,
loving to read Italian and Greek:
I knew they would take him away with bare hands.
He would not see the eagle sharpen its beak.'

Mandelstam is dreaming of rosewood and halva,
and the wild gorges of Armenia, where
his words tasted of wood smoke. He wakes
into the teasing of his wide-lipped angel.

Her huge blue eyes are slant, her mouth sensual.
His upper lip is twitching with displeasure,
but then he laughs, like a toothless baby,
and falls across the bed with his arms around her.

You can hear a guitar from a neighbour's flat.
He and Nadezhda are living gaily together.
He was afraid of oysters and the bark of a dog;
he never let himself drink unboiled water.

So how was it he chose to read that
poem aloud to so many
friends, knowing the danger
of a knock on the door, arrest and the Lubianka?

13 Voronezh

The charming domestic game is over. The flat with its books and papers has disappeared. We are in another climate. A fairytale winter in Voronezh. Calm. Cracking frost. Blue snow.

Mandelstam is allowed to live in any town more than 100 kilometres away from Moscow. But he has been mad, and is still ill; his asthma is bad; at night he struggles to breathe and has to sleep propped up on pillows. He and Nadezhda have no money for food. Their room is a glassed-over veranda in a large, rundown house.

On the narrow, crooked streets, he is stared at, and suspected. His eyelashes are gone, and his eyelids red; the snow scalds his eyes. He does not have the physiology for heroism. In the Lubianka he recited the poem about Stalin to his captors at once. They had a copy anyway.

The pathos of memory.

Sometimes he imagines himself in The Stray Dog, at a side table with Akhmatova. There is a scarf thrown across her shoulders. Her hair is drawn back harshly; her tender mouth and huge grey eyes are sombre. She is smoking one cigarette after another. When Mandelstam takes the stage to read a poem, he walks with his head thrown back, a lily of the valley in his buttonhole. The room stills to listen. As he returns to the table, Akhmatova's eyes darken and she whispers to him.

'Most poetry is so boring. But when you read, Osip …'

They are not lovers. She has teased him out of that. He offers his love instead to Princess Salomea Andronikova, his Solominka, and allows himself to break his heart over her beauty.

He does not recall the first days of Revolution, or the Civil War. What he remembers is a sanatorium in Detskoye Selo some years later. Nadezhda is sitting on a veranda in March, huddled under heavy blankets. She is taking her temperature every hour of the day. When the doctors shake their heads, he becomes agitated and questions them until she begs him to stop. He is so deeply in love, he stays in a nearby *pension* to be with her, even though he dislikes the landscape of straggly grey trees.

He asks her advice on every word of his poetry.

Akhmatova sits in another deckchair close by. She has had tuberculosis since childhood; the years of the Moscow famine have made her dangerously thin. The two women gossip about Akhmatova's current lover, Nikolai Punin. To Mandelstam, Nadezhda repeats with delight Akhmatova's ironic words: 'Men are always so charming and considerate when they come courting.'

When Nadezhda is sturdy enough, she and Osip make for Moscow even though his work is no longer sought after and they have nowhere to live. For a time, they lodge with Emma Gerstein, whose father is a consultant in a good hospital and therefore has a large flat. Mandelstam lets grey stubble grow on his cheeks, neglects his health and wears crumpled collars. No lily of the valley in his lapel now. They allow the room they occupy to fall into squalid disorder. No one wants his poetry. It is like meeting a posterity which has already forgotten him, has no need of him, would prefer not to consider what has become of him.

'It's hard to move between people pretending to be alive,'

he remarks, referring to the local editors of journals and those who control the publishing houses.

It is Nadezhda who secures their miraculous flat in Nashchokin Lane by dragging a mattress into it before any rivals. For a time they are happy there. They set out favourite books. Entertain friends.

Akhmatova often stays with them. And she is there when they come to arrest him: still calm, strong and generous. He had begged and boiled a single egg from a neighbour for her supper. While the NKVD begin their searches and announce they have a warrant for his arrest, she gives the egg back to him, saying he will need all his strength. He peels it, puts salt on it and eats it.

In the Lubianka, he confesses everything at once. They tortured him nevertheless: with bright lights and lack of sleep. The screams they told him were Nadezhda's sent him mad. Even in Cherdyn high in the Urals he has hallucinations about her suffering. And Akhmatova too: he imagines her thrown down a cliff, and calling for help.

Here in Voronezh, his lips move as he walks. Sometimes he is writing poems. Sometimes he talks to an invisible companion, perhaps Gumilyov, Akhmatova's first husband, shot by the Bolsheviks more than ten years ago.

'Nikolai,' he murmurs. 'We were right. Only *things* are real. Forget symbols and mysticism. All a poet needs is an axe head. Starlight. A frozen rain butt. Nikolai. My friend. Are you there? There are not many people I can talk to when Nadezhda goes to Moscow. It is a pity that you are dead.

'You cannot write to the dead. And the living often don't reply either. I think of my brother as a child in the Tenishev School in St Petersburg. We played soccer in shorts, wool socks and English blouses, and were taught the Anglo-

Saxon virtues. I remember the heavy, sweetish smell of gas in the laboratories, the snowball fights in the playground. Everything else I had to find out for myself. Our childhood loyalties. Now, dear brother, you write that you can send me no money. You plead your own family responsibilities. As if I were not your family.

'It was my mother who arranged the Tenishev school. She knew what she wanted for us. And she spoke the Russian language in all its purity. I knew Pushkin in her voice. The excitement of that. Even now, when I talk about Pushkin, Nadya has to take my pulse. My father still had a thick Polish accent; a prosperous Warsaw leather merchant barely out of the ghetto. His German was good, though; he could read Goethe, was in love with German philosophy. I see him in his top hat and synagogue clothes hustling us all into a carriage for the September Holy Days.

'I did not even know the letters of the prayer book. My grandfather covered my shoulders with a yellow shawl, and was disappointed in me. I did not like the odours of my grandparents' house, the closed-in mustiness of their small rooms. And their food was spiced too strongly for my taste. My father's study, too, was an alien world, with a Turkish couch covered with ledgers of flimsy paper, and bookshelves of Hebrew books not stacked side by side but thrown together one on top of the other every which way.

'Strange what comes to mind. Just now I remembered the Jewish quarter in Petersburg just behind the Mariinski Theatre. On Tergovaya Street. The synagogue has conical caps, onion domes and an exotic fig tree. You could see shop signs in spiky script, and Jewish women with false hair poking out under their headscarves.

'To become a Russian poet, you have to give up all that rubbish. When I went to St Petersburg University, I let myself be baptised without a qualm. I was giving my allegiance to Christian Art and the Russian calendar: decorated eggs, Christmas trees. The Jewish festivals of Rosh Hashanah and Yom Kippur were harsh sounds in my ear. A commonplace treachery, irrelevant now in our new Soviet world where no religion is allowed.

'So much simpler to love the Lutheran Church, however, not the Russian Orthodox. My only regret, now, is losing the melody of Yiddish. I did not hear it at home. I learned that music only from the genius of Solomon Mikhoels. Late. Late in my life. In the Yiddish State Theatre. How can I describe the charm of the language? It has an upward curve; the sentences are interrogative, and yet somehow disappointed at the same time. Such absurd lines Mikhoels could make with his body, how elegant he was.

'It was in Kiev I saw him first. A magician. He created his own props: a needle and thread, a glass of pepper-vodka. In Kiev, a city of golden domes and pogroms, with candles in the chestnut trees and the down of lindens in the air. The city where I found my love. If you take a tram to the Podol where the Jews and gangsters live, you will think it the liveliest part of the city, but remember: the Podol has often been set in flames. The Podol has often flooded. But any Jew is fragile as porcelain. I doubt Mikhoels will survive.'

For a moment, Mandelstam is silent. The path is steeper and he has to pause to catch his breath.

Nadezhda is in Moscow, finding work as a translator. Without her earnings they could not eat. But he needs her with him. When she is away, he has attacks of panic. Will there be a telegram from Nadya today? Their last telephone call, he was shamefully quarrelsome. He did not even thank her for the roubles she had wired at the beginning of the

58

week. She is working too hard, his angel. She should be here at his side. Sudden anxiety for her clutches like an unfriendly hand on the airsacs of his lungs.

Madness to hang around Moscow in 1937 without the right to live there. She tries to sell his work, but editors are not interested in him. His surname does him no good. At *Noviy Mir* someone suggests he change his Jewish surname to something more Russian.

There is no telegram. Wildly, extravagantly, he writes to her, sending his love, apologies and desperation, and leaves himself no money for the fuel he will need tomorrow.

Back in the room, he makes a fire with the wood that is left. The effort makes him wheeze. He glances up from time to time with a quick, almost furtive glance, as if he sensed an alien presence. But as he huddles in front of the flames drowsily it is Nadezhda he talks to.

'This is Voronezh, in the region of the Black Earth. There are ravens in the name of that city, can you hear them? And a robber's knife. Rooks scatter like flicks of burnt sugar across the sky. The houses are painted pistachio green. I can fly and sing, but I crawl along these streets afraid to fall in a snow drift.'

When his temperature begins to rise, he dreams of hot fresh bread, pine baths and a river flowing into an inky forest. Or an open window in the Podol, where he can make out a loaf of *challah* bread, some herring and some tea. No. Moscow is his home now; he longs to be back in the flat on Nashchokin Lane. But not St Petersburg. *To live in St Petersburg is like living in a coffin.*

He moans in his sleep.

'I cannot bear to be alone. Nadenka. Nadenka, my breathing is difficult if you are not here with me. Only with you am I able to draw breath normally. Without you I suffocate. I am a shadow. I do not exist. Who will visit me?'

It is a long train journey from Moscow to Voronezh. Akhmatova made the trip once. It took thirty-six hours, she said. And my brother did not even buy pillows or blankets for her. She endured the discomfort without complaint. When we met, we were both like ghosts, but after a while there was laughter again. Electricity. Perhaps too much electricity?

There are moments of happiness even for a disgraced poet. A hand is waking him. It is Nadezhda, dressed in her beret and a short leather jacket, who has come from the train and sets her bags on the carpet. She is down-to-earth and unladylike, and he holds on to her like a baby.

She explains there is no good news; she no longer dares to speak to friends in case she incriminates them. But she has brought money for the week's food and more. He tells her about the sanatorium where they treated the frostbite on his ears with the dark-blue light of a quartz lamp. She soothes him but even so they come close to quarrelling when he says, matter of factly, without rancour:

'Aren't you ashamed? You'll write memoirs about me after I am dead but you don't care enough to stay here and look after me.'

They are soon wrapped deeply in one another's arms, and begin the whispering reminiscence of a long marriage.

Tsvetaeva puts her hands over her ears. 'I do not want to hear them talk of me. I know why he left me, of course, but I don't want to hear Nadya reminding him how badly I behaved, how I ignored her, how rudely I took him to see Alya as if he belonged to me. I know, and I don't want to stay here any longer.'

14 The innocence of Isaac Babel

Among so many pale, bewildered ghosts
    one sturdy figure beckons. Clean-shaven,
eyes glinting behind heavy lenses;
    his smile a cat-triangle.

He has seen white roads, old waggoners,
    and riff-raff living on raw carrots;
slept on the dirt floor of poor villages
    pretending not to know Yiddish;

felt the shame of his own *rachmones*,
    derided by Budyonny's bold Asiatics,
and still tethered his horse under the trees,
    of four-hundred-year-old cemeteries.

He rode with godless adrenalin
    flooding his body,
and his soul was filled
    with love of food and women,

but there was nothing mean or crabby in him.
    He gave away his watch, his shirts,
his ties: to have possessions was to make a gift of them.
    His being touches anyone who listens.

15 Peredelkino, May 1939

It is 16 May 1939, a warm spring day with birdsong. There are green trees and plum blossoms. Isaac Babel is asleep in his dacha. He is a child running along streets he does not recognise. His face is wet and salty. The streets are empty, the shops boarded up. At a distance, he makes out gunfire, then silence. It is a lonely dream, a dream of loneliness.

As he rises towards waking, he feels for his wife, then remembers she is in Moscow at his apartment on the Lane of Great Nicola and the Sparrows. Nina. He thinks of her sturdy body, her calm intelligence, her beauty. He is lucky. Women like him. They always have, even though he has glasses and a growing paunch. He makes them laugh. Even when they are angry they like to sleep with him.

He remembers the plot of land he bought on a steep embankment overlooking the sea in Odessa. As he thinks of Odessa, he is homesick. 'One day,' he tells Nina in his dream, 'we will build on it. We shall drink tea with apples, and shop for bagels. Moscow is cold and sunless most of the year, but in Odessa you can throw off your clothes and swim in the sea.'

The covers are light, and we can make out the weight of Babel's shoulders. He is a powerful man. In his dream, he is a horseman riding over a world of grass in July heat. He is riding with Kuban Cossacks, reckless men, who loot the little Jewish towns they pass, help themselves to potatoes, meat, recently baked cakes. The Ukraine is in flames. There are streets of blazing shacks. Old men. Screaming women. The wounded in bandages with bare bellies. Bewildered

63

Jews dishevelled in waistcoats and without socks. Fear.

Then there is a bang on the bedroom door. He is suddenly altogether awake. He can taste his own sweat as he licks his lips.

'Who's there?'

Who else would it be? He has been waiting for them.

Nina is with two men. They allow Babel to dress but, as he emerges from the bedroom, they order him to put up his hands as if they were all part of an American gangster film. They go through his pockets. There is loose money, not much, a pencil, a few scraps of paper. Nina comes to sit next to him, and takes his hands. They huddle together. He breathes in her presence gratefully. She smells sweetly familiar.

The men work quickly. All his papers and files are tied into bundles and taken away. Nina tells him the NKVD have already raided his Moscow flat. They were there before daybreak.

'You don't get much sleep in your line of work, do you?' Babel teases one of the men.

Nobody laughs. Humour is not encouraged in the NKVD.

Nina squeezes his fingers. She does not want him to antagonise these officers of the law. He smiles at her innocence, her credulity. She imagines a few words or a wry smile are relevant to men who have their orders and have not asked to understand them. She does not yet believe there is torture in Soviet prisons.

The men allow Nina to travel with him in the car on the way to Moscow. Babel kisses her ear, and whispers into her hair.

'See my daughter grows up happy. Let André know what has happened.'

He means Malraux. Perhaps he can help? He knows he will need all the help he can muster.

'You will be all right,' he reassures Nina, nevertheless. 'A brilliant engineer? Always useful. Who needs writers, especially if they don't write?'

She is very strong. She does not cry, but she does not laugh either. When they say goodbye, with a long hard kiss, he knows it is over.

Except for the pain.

Inside the Lubianka, he gives up his passport, the keys to his flat and laces from his shoes. His fingerprints are taken. He is escorted to a cell in a yellow building within the Lubianka's inner courtyard. He knows his interrogators will be men who left school at eleven, who have never read a book, who do not know or care who he is, only that he has been designated an enemy.

He is not allowed soap, shaving material, braces or garters. They want him to grow filthy and unshaven until they are ready to question him. One of them snaps his glasses and then grinds them under his feet on the floor. Babel peers round blindly. Helpless. He remembers Yagoda's advice about what to do if arrested: *Admit nothing. Then our interrogators are powerless.* Not reliable advice evidently, since Yagoda himself is already dead, taken out and shot in 1938 after a year in a cell and some part in the show trials.

Babel knows about the 'conveyor belt'. Teams of fresh interrogators allow a prisoner no respite. They will beat the soles of his feet and the base of his spine and deprive him of sleep. They will threaten his family. Everyone confesses. The brave leaders of the Revolution, Stalin's comrades –

Zinoviev, Kamenev – all confessed their treachery. Publicly. And his own friend and long-time protector, Bukharin? Stalin insisted Ehrenburg watch Bukharin's trial. He obeyed and was almost destroyed by what he saw. He never wrote about it. Never spoke of what he had seen. *There are some things a decent man does not report.*

Babel tells himself: I was always a loyal Bolshevik. I believed in the Revolution. In Lenin. In the Red Army. That's why I rode alongside the Cossacks. We were going to overturn the injustice of the Tsars. On which other side should I fight? He stares at the ceiling as he waits.

In the *stetl*, people spoke of going to live like a god in Odessa. We escaped from the *stetl*, cut off our sidelocks and turned to Revolution and Poetry. And it has come to this. Nothing has changed since they first destroyed the Temple. Misha Yaponchik, the model for Benya Krik, helped defend Odessa Jews from the Whites in the Civil War. He was murdered by the Reds.

They have taken away Babel's watch, and he does not know how much time has passed. His voice goes on in his head, in the long silence. Several days' silence. He is not a *shtarker*, a tough guy, for all his solidity. His body is middle-aged, over-indulged, out of condition. Not that it makes any difference to his situation.

He does not wonder why the NKVD have come for him. They have taken away so many of his friends. He had been one of the privileged of the Writers' Union. They gave him a big Ford, a chauffeur, allowed him to eat at 'closed' restaurants and travel wherever he wanted inside the Soviet Union. This was remarkably good fortune for an inventor of fairytales, an impudent trickster who has fallen silent. His bluff has been called. What else could he expect?

Without glasses, his face looks meek and vulnerable, as if he were once again a shy, myopic child, with asthma. A sensitive boy who wanted to own a pair of doves. He misses his little French daughter Natasha. He would have liked to walk with her up Deribasovskaya in the sunshine, but he knows that will not happen now. For a moment, he thinks of his first wife, who has never forgiven his infidelity, or the son he had with another woman.

What has he believed in? He remembers the rabbis of his childhood, their instructions, their myths. No comfort there. Has he lived a wicked life? They would say so. But he has been kind and cheerful. Mine is an animal nature, he reflects. Plump women. Fine horses. Ice cream on a hot day. Laughter.

The walls of the unheated cell are damp, and he shivers. There will be no merriment here. In a moment they will bring some swill, and he will eat it. He knows what it is to fight for breath, to be afraid, to be humiliated. What happens in this cellar will be far worse. They are leaving him here alone so that he will understand as much.

In the silence, his thoughts drift and focus.

People will say I am here because I was once the lover of Yezhov's wife. It may be so. Yezhov, that evil dwarf, master of the Terror. Yes, I saw the hatred in his eyes when I visited his flat. Even though my love affair with Yevgenia was long over, and I went to those literary salons of hers as rarely as possible. Last winter she poisoned herself. Who knows why? Even Stalin was puzzled. Or so they say. Yezhov was removed from his post in January 1939. He is already dead, but words can damage from beyond the grave.

Babel falls asleep sitting up, and dreams of the French writer André Malraux with dark blond hair, and a lock falling over his forehead. Malraux seems to shake his head sorrowfully. Babel tells him: 'When Gorky died, I knew they were not going to let me live.'

What seems most bitter when he wakes is remembering that he has begun to work again. The quiet of the dacha in Peredelkino suited him. There were no close neighbours. His rooms were almost unfurnished. He slept on a simple wooden plank with a mattress. He had low bookcases without ornaments, and a leather-seated chair bought from a junk shop. All he needed. Every morning he has been getting up early, eager to write. Short stories. He spent the last few evenings in his dacha translating Sholem Aleichem from Yiddish. In Moscow there were too many disturbances. The telephone rang too frequently: he sometimes put his little daughter Lidia on the line to say he was not home. Or imitated a female voice himself. His house had always been full of visitors; many writers he was too kind to discourage; now the wives of those arrested came to him for help. He soothed them as well as he could. Sometimes he invented stories to give them hope. Even at the end of 1938, it was not yet certain that 'ten years without benefit of correspondence' was a euphemism for execution.

'They didn't let me finish,' Babel says aloud in the empty cell. It is not clear whether he is talking about the stories he was working on or his own life. Probably no one is listening.

How can he declare himself a traitor to the Soviet Union?

The human body is vulnerable to many kinds of pain. You can put a man's head in a bucket of water and watch him gasp for breath; hang him from tied arms until his shoulders crack; whip the soles of his feet. Attach electrodes to his genitals. If you don't care whether he survives, you can kick him with your heavy boots until his spleen ruptures and his spine breaks.

The torturers know: anyone can be broken.

When he has confessed, they take him back to his cellar.

Then the door is kicked open and his heart bangs. Have they come for him again? But no, they are bringing him new trousers and a shirt. In the pocket is a handkerchief heavily perfumed with Nina's favourite scent. He inhales deeply with closed eyes. Happiness. Gaiety. Another world.

When they bring him to Lavrenti Beria's office, the trial takes less than ten minutes.

It is a small room. Tsvetaeva and I are there, pressed against the wall, but no one is aware of our presence. Babel is brought in, filthy and unshaven. Without his glasses, he can barely make out the man behind the desk. Since he cannot see, his balance is impaired. He blinks and staggers. No one helps him.

'Why do you think you have been brought here?'

'It is my inability to write.'

'What, you think you are arrested as an author? Think again.'

'Perhaps because I went abroad?'

'Surely you realise we want to learn about your activity as a spy? You and Yevgenia Yezhova worked together. We want to know about the rest of your network.'

'There is no network. Neither of us were spies.'

'Understand me. We want the details. We shall have them soon enough. Why do you force us to hurt you?'

As he is taken away, he lifts his head as if his blindness has strengthened some other sense. As if he felt there were spectres present from another age.

The guard pushes him out of the door. We do not follow him to his cell. Instead, we walk in the sunshine.

We are in another, darker room. Babel is much thinner. His face is bruised, a blow has closed his right eye, his front teeth are broken. One of his legs trails behind him awkwardly as he peers at his interrogator. But when he speaks, his voice is firm.

'I want to confess a crime, committed while I was in prison.'

The interrogator looks surprised. Babel holds on to the back of a chair.

'In prison? Strange. Don't worry about it. You have already admitted your guilt.'

'I do not consider myself guilty. Except for this – during the interrogation I made up everything I said about the theatre director Solomon Mikhoels, the great film director Sergei Eisenstein. And Ilya Ehrenburg.'

'Why would you lie? About such serious matters?'

'Out of cowardice. To please my questioners. The Court must decide. The point is, there is no truth in what I said. They are all loyal Soviet citizens. I have no hope now for myself but I cannot bear to bring trouble on my friends.'

'The Court will make up its own mind about that. And do you also deny your foreign ties?'

'My ties, as you call them, were never more than writers' friendships.'

'We know better. You set up a monthly journal. With André Gide, whose anti-Soviet views are well known. You worked as a French spy for Malraux, giving him information about our aviation. Didn't you?'

'The journal came to nothing. You must know Malraux is a friend of the Soviet Union. What military information could I give him anyway? What do I know about aviation? Only things he could read himself in the newspapers.'

'And Yevgenia Yezhova?'

'I have told you. We have hardly spoken in years. Never in private.'

'Yezhov said he heard about your plotting from his wife herself. He had no reason to lie. Why should he be jealous when she assured him you have never been lovers? She was afraid of you, because of what you knew. Because of the plots you had hatched together.'

'An implausible invention.'

'We have signed testimony.'

'Sadly, both your witnesses are dead, I think. A problem to confront them, even if you were willing to let me do so. I suppose that is often the way.'

Leaning forward, the interrogator gives a blow to Babel's face that pitches him to the floor, before calling a minion.

'Take him back to his cell.'

Tsvetaeva murmurs to me: *Babel loved the Revolution and believed in it, and then it murdered him. It was in January 1940. The theatre director Meyerhold was shot in the same week. The bodies were taken away to the cemetery in the old Donskoi monastery in the middle of Moscow, and tipped into a common grave.*

As she is speaking, we pass through the gate into Lubianka Square. In the centre stands the statue of Feliks Dzerzhinsky on its column. We look back at the façade of yellow brick. The prison is handsome in the sunshine. There is a clock in the uppermost band of the façade, under a small cupola. On the third floor, the windows of Lavrenti Beria, the current Head of the Secret Police, look down on us.

16 Cherry brandy, May 1938

Osip and Nadezhda nuzzle together
like two blind puppies. No more
fortunes to be told in wax.
They are safe and warm,
in Samatikha, a rest home near Murom.

Pear and cherry blossom rustle
in the warm air. Frogs jump happily.
Osip and Nadezhda are still
asleep, tasting the sweet, hot
intoxication of the night before.

For May Day, there is to be ice cream,
and in town the celebrations will be noisy.
But Nadezhda dreams of icons
from the nearby Saviour monastery,
and wakes in cold terror.

Osip makes fun of the ill omen: the worst
of their troubles are past history. Here
they have found shelter. So both of them
are still in night clothes, and unprepared,
when the soldiers come to take him away.

17 Barracks No. 11, Vladivostok 1938

Mandelstam is lying in what looks like a heap of old rags. If he had ever had mittens to protect his hands from the cold, they have been stolen weeks ago. His white, bloodless fingers are long and his overgrown nails filthy. He is tossing feverishly on his bunk, the lower of two, with someone still snoring above him. The blankets stink. There are several other men waking in the unheated shack with thick ice on the windows. Intermittently, a yellow searchlight outside lights up the stubbly faces. Some of them raise their heads, but they are staring at Mandelstam not me. Someone called out for him to stop muttering. It was as if I did not exist for anyone else.

From time to time the muscles of his face contract in an involuntary spasm. At first I cannot make out his blurred words. But suddenly he says with perfect clarity:

'I'm in very poor health. Exhausted. But at least I wasn't picked for Kolyma.'

Kolyma is a frozen camp of the Gulag in the far north-east of Siberia, where conditions were so harsh few prisoners survived a month. Kolyma meant death.

Sometimes men remember their childhood in their last days, sometimes their whole past life seems like a dream and only their present pains have any reality. He remembers words he has written in a letter.

'Here I am, a toothless old Zek in a transit camp without felt boots.'

He looks at me narrowly.

'You look fit and well. Are you some kind of relative I have forgotten? My brother Zhenya decided long ago that my life was not worth much to him. He doesn't give a damn about me. I wrote as much. I told him. Do not dare to call yourself my brother. So what do *you* want with me? Do you bring soup or bread?'

I shake my head.

'Then what use are you? Do we share the same disease? It is what brought me here. I can remember walking along Kamen Ostrovsky Boulevard, over the bridge, by the Winter Palace. That was when I understood. Once you are in trouble, nobody phones. Nobody visits. The books also die. They are taken out of libraries. People are afraid to own copies in their own homes.'

Another angry voice from further down the barracks rises to demand his silence. These were the last precious minutes before a guard would appear. Moments in which the prisoners could dream.

For a moment, Mandelstam is silent too, remembering.

'Nadenka. My bird. My little rabbit,' he whispers. 'Sometimes I hear you breathing at my side, and talking to me in your sleep. But I am alone here. Everything that has happened is irreparable.'

He began to mumble again, as if his energy had given out. His voice was once again almost inaudible. His thoughts scatter.

'I know the hell we make for each other on earth. But I am not afraid to believe in Paradise. We shall be together there, Nadenka.'

He begins to talk about Parnok, in *The Egyptian Stamp*, with his shiny little shoes like black sheep hooves, who tried to phone the police to stop a lynching. A hoarse rattling laugh almost drowns his voice, but I recognise the story, written years before his first arrest. His last spluttering words come out clearly enough:

'He might as well have tried to telephone Persephone.'

In the pause, I think frantically how to assure him that his writing would live on but he stops me mid-sentence.

'I am not a writer, because I never write. I have no manuscripts, no notebooks. I worked as I walked. Mumbling. Learning my own words. To be a writer here in Russia is not compatible with the honourable title of Jew, do you understand?'

Suddenly he seemed to rouse himself, and said distinctly: 'I still want to be tried. Are the legal proceedings at an end?' Then he fell back and said no more, though he still appeared to be breathing.

As daylight began to come in through the windows, guards appeared with rye bread on plywood trays. They seemed as unaware of my presence as the other prisoners had been, though one looked at me and crossed himself, as if made uneasy in a way he could not understand.

18 Strangers

Weightless shadows in the chilly sunshine.
    Among them, a figure I recognise
with a black felt hat pulled over
    a long chin, bushy eyebrows and large eyes.

It is Faina Ranevskaya, comic genius,
    Akhmatova's Charlie Chaplin, met
in Tashkent under apricot trees.
    She introduces herself in a hoarse voice.

'My father was a rich synagogue elder
    in Taganrog. When I wanted to be an actress,
he advised me, *Look in the mirror, daughter.*
    Those words still hurt, even in my success.

Yes, I was famous. Yes, I was not poor.
    But if only you knew my loneliness.
Damn the talent made me so unhappy.
    My friend Akhmatova was always a beauty

but sorrowful, although we laughed together.
    We were much of an age. I, too,
could still remember decent people then
    – Lord, how old that makes me.

She died before my own heart attack,
    and so I never had the chance to tell her:
'Even Soviet doctors are powerless,
    if the patient wants to recover.'

As Faina laughs, a darker figure shoulders
    her aside, and grips me with the fingers
of a skeleton. 'I am *Der Nister*,'
    he says. 'The Secret One.

I speak for generations of believers
    in the God your grandfather knew.
They settled in their *stetls* west of Kiev
    and could not leave like you.'

19 Stetl

Rechytsa was my great-grandfather Hatskell's *stetl*. It was not as large as Berdichev, or Zhitomir; the town never held more than ten thousand people. Polish, Lithuanian and Russian Empires flowed over Belarus and the Jews of Rechytsa went on living by their own calendar of feasts and fasts. In Hatskell's day the little town was modestly prosperous. Turkish goods came in on river boats along the Dnepr. Rye and wheat were brought in from neighbouring villages. Their Gentile neighbours were often emancipated serfs who usually paid for their goods with a goose or a pot of honey.

The Jews understood their poverty – there were many poor Jews in Rechytsa – but were alarmed by their savagery. There were tales of public whippings, thieves dragged through the streets behind a horse. Their drunkenness, too, was frightening, their vodka poisonous; their anger against oppression only too often directed against the Jews.

In the only photograph I have of Hatskell, he is wearing a dark, buttoned overcoat and a bowler hat. He has no curling sidelocks. No caftan. His moustache is black, and his grey beard neatly trimmed. His face is broad and his features even, his eyes neither large nor melancholy, his expression determined. He is said to have been a factor for a large landowner and to have travelled as far as St Petersburg on business. I don't know. Other members of the family were in the wood trade. The family was conventionally pious but fervent piety was on the wane in his time. Neither his own wife, nor the wives of his sons, wore wigs. They were believers, but not fanatic, though the women remained superstitious, often influenced by Russian customs, throwing spilt salt over the left shoulder, or spitting to turn away the Evil Eye. The family observed the Sabbath, attended the synagogue, ate kosher food, but Hatskell was no follower of Rabbi Nachman of Bratslav, with his offer of mystic redemption through suffering. The family continued to have some faith in God's protection. Once, when I was sitting on Zaida's knee, I remember asking him whether he was afraid of dying. He shrugged and pointed at the ceiling. 'He will look after me,' he said. 'He always has.'

There are few signs of God's protection in Rechytsa. It is one of the towns where the Jews were massacred by the Cossack hero, Bogdan Khmelnitsky, in the seventeenth century, and the history of south-east Belarus continued to be murderous through the centuries that followed. Once the Jewish population made up half the little town. In the twenty-first century there are no Jews, and few signs Jews ever lived there. Soviet policy destroyed their synagogues and *yeshivas* even before the Germans arrived to kill all those who could not run away.

A traveller passing through Rechytsa in Hatskell's day would see dirt, puddles and small houses, their roofs mouldy and hung with swallow nests. Some only had floors of earth. The young always wanted to leave. Why would anyone want to stay in Rechytsa? But travel was expensive, and in any case Jews were not allowed to leave the Pale of Settlement. Soon, early marriage and children anchored them. Except for Hatskell's son, Menachem Mendl, my Zaida, who was sent south to Odessa to study in a *yeshiva*.

I am not sure what Zaida was really doing in Odessa. In some stories he worked on the docks, unloading fish. In others his wife worked in a factory while he studied in the *yeshiva*. He was certainly a learned man. He understood Rashi; he could quote from Akiba. He could read and write five languages, though he preferred to speak Yiddish. But he was no businessman and had no feeling for the wood trade. He was a dreamer. A man who loved Ecclesiastes more than any other book in the canon, relished good food, sweet wine and laughter, and believed money came and went at God's whim.

Zaida left Odessa with his young wife and first child, not in flight from a pogrom but to avoid conscription. Service in the Tsar's army was often a death sentence for a Jew. Leaving Russia wasn't easy. My aunt Eva, Zaida's first child, told me how they had to bribe a guard to let the family cross the border and that their apprehensions continued all the way to Berlin. The family lived in Berlin for a time, in the last decade of the nineteenth century, and then shifted again, to London. When I asked him why he moved on, he said it was because the English believed in fair play.

Mendl's brothers followed him to England and then to Canada, a venture which was disastrous since he knew little about farming and the land near Montreal is frozen for more than six months of the year. It took months of hard work to earn enough for the whole family to return to England, but they fared well, whether in Liverpool, Manchester or London, surviving largely through a willingness to work long hours. Brothers, sons and daughters alike kept the enterprise going, and no one else was given the time to brood over books as Mendl was.

Rechytsa still sits on the steep right bank of the Dnepr, but Hatskell's direct descendants have long ago dispersed to the United States, Argentina, Canada, Uruguay, South Africa. Uncles, cousins, in-laws and their numerous progeny who remained in Belarus were less fortunate. Many in Rechytsa welcomed the Revolution, which emancipated them from Tsarist discrimination, at least on paper. But in the Civil War the Red armies turned out to be almost as brutal as the White. Jews who owned stores or factories found themselves in particular trouble; even those who set out their goods in baskets on market days, or hung a string of salt fish, a cluster of bagels or a wreath of Turkish peppers over their doors were designated class enemies. Plunder was commonplace. So were murder and rape.

When Stalin made his pact with Hitler, all Jews were afraid but, mysteriously, other pressures began to ease. Who knew why? The Ukraine was fertile, seeds sown in 1940 meant there was bread. There was even fruit and vegetables. Rechytsa lived in a dream of restored plenty.

And into that dream I wander, on my own, without Tsvetaeva to guide me.

There are horses in the fields of the collective farms. They swish their tails to keep off the flies. The air is sweet with the scents of early summer. The dusty road that leads to the *stetl* is quiet and I walk along it as if back into my own past

It is 1941. On the narrow streets of the town the stall-keepers are drinking tea together, and I listen to them complain about a consignment of vegetables from the Ukraine, and the scraggy hens. Some fall into Yiddish, but most speak Russian, with a nasal burr. These are poor people, gentle people.

In the streets, many children are chasing one another, their shrieks regarded tolerantly. A toddler falls in a puddle and a man lifts him up. His clothes are filthy but the man soothes him without reproach until he stops crying. A woman comes out and shouts angrily at him.

What are they doing? What is their work? These Jews of Rechytsa are strange to me. It is a foreign landscape. Suddenly, rounding a twist in a lane, I make out a wood shop, open to the street. And the smells are familiar. Creosote, wood shavings and boiling glue. I remember sitting as a school child in my father's factory, smelling those same pungent odours. I can even hear the whine of a circular saw. Inside, behind an open door, a large-boned woman with flashing eyes, red cheeks and brawny upper arms looks up as I look in. We stare at one another.

She could be my Aunt Clara, who ran her own wood shop in Manchester. A handsome woman, rather larger than her husband. Behind both of them sits an old man – white haired, much the age Zaida would have been in 1941. He looks less benevolent, however. Less bookish. More formidable even though he is close to sleep, his mouth sunken over his few teeth. He comes to wakefulness abruptly. His eyes are bright in his narrow face. Everyone looks at me, and for the first time in my travels I know I am not invisible.

My presence puzzles them. I remember that bewilderment from the time I was driven north to meet my aunts in Manchester long ago. It is as if I have become a child of six again, with olive skin and black eyes, unmistakeably part of the gene pool but yet a stranger.

They speak in a warm, hasty Yiddish.

'Who does she look like?'

'One of the Bobroff family. A cousin from Kovno.'

They all have their suggestions.

'She looks hungry,' the young man says.

As he turns, I recognise a fleeting resemblance to my own father. Something in the skew of the smile, something in the straight black hair combed back from his forehead, something in the ease with which he handles machinery. He is as deft and practical as Menachem Mendl had been unworldly.

'Do you want some soup?' he asks me. 'Hannah, give her some soup.'

The woman beckons me in.

'Where do you come from?'

I shake my head. How can I answer that? She takes me through anyway into the kitchen that lies behind the workshop. It is a cramped space, with another large woman at the other side of the table, rolling pastry. When she has finished, she wipes her hands on her apron and begins to cut the flat pastry into little squares. For *mandels*, I remember suddenly, those delicious fried squares of dough which my own mother put into soup. The first woman, seeing my interest, takes down a jar from the only shelf and offers me a handful to taste. Hannah puts a bowl of chicken soup in front of me. As if hypnotised by my arrival, both the old man and Hannah's husband follow into the already crowded room.

'We keep hens,' Hannah tells me. She is proud of it. Her cheeks are red with the excitement of it, and she laughs boldly. 'Sometimes they are stolen.'

'The *Goyim*,' the old man says.

I am beginning to realise that the room I had thought of as a kitchen is the only room on the ground floor. Stairs lead out of it into the next storey and a back door leads to the yard.

'Russian peasants steal anything that moves. Eat anything that moves.'

'Not only the *Goyim*,' the woman reproaches him. 'But of course we don't usually eat our hens. We keep them for the eggs. I collect them early in the morning, before the lazy buggers wake up. But this is an old fowl. And tonight is the Sabbath.' She smiles. 'Old fowls make the best soup.'

Then the white-haired old man fits tin glasses to his nose, the better to survey me, and then gives that Eastern European shrug which can mean whatever you want it to mean. In this case it seems to mean: it doesn't matter who she is, she is hungry, let her eat.

Because it is almost summer, I have not noticed the light going but the sun is now behind a house across the street. Although it looks impossible for a single extra human body to push itself into the room, several children rush in, many of them with black hair and faces as narrow as my own. They stare at me.

Then the woman who had been rolling the pastry comes in, apologising without fuss for her lateness. She has changed her blouse, and looks unflustered; the only one among them with long yellow hair. I saw she was the beauty of the family and that even the old man regarded her indulgently.

The room is becoming unbearably hot. Hannah lights candles in two stubby candlesticks. The old man says prayers from memory. He cuts a piece of the plaited loaf, which is covered with a white cloth. We all share it, and then a glass of sweet red wine is passed round the table. It is too sweet for me, and I am becoming faint and a little nauseous.

The chicken soup is much too hot, with burning fat glistening on the surface. I blow on my spoon. The last time I remember scalding my lips on such soup, it was at the house of my Aunt Eva in Neasden, a cultured woman who loved music. As I remember her, she had a handsome, dimpled face and reddened her lips even in her nineties. All her children played a musical instrument.

Emboldened by that memory, I tell them:

'I am a grandchild of Menachem Mendl. Do you remember him? He was one of Hatskell's children.'

'Hatskell?' The young man smiles. 'My father's uncle? I am named for him. In my passport, my name is Yevgeny Azimov. But in this house I am known as Hatskell ben Efraim. I never knew him, of course. They say he followed his sons abroad.'

And then there is a knock on the door. For a moment the family scene freezes. Is their enterprise legal, I wonder? Are people allowed to trade on their own, or is everything under the control of some invisible Soviet? But when Hannah rises to let in the visitor, they welcome the newcomer with shrieks of delight. Is he a cousin, or an elder brother? A cousin, I decide, noting his well-cut hair and neatly shaven face. They hail him as Abram, but he rebukes them. He has changed his name. They must learn to use the new one. Mikhail Kuznetsov. He has come from Kiev, where life goes on splendidly and there is no longer any prejudice against Jews.

They laugh at that, and he looks a little offended, but sits down at the table nonetheless. He is married now, but has not brought his wife. She is fully Russian and he does not want any embarrassment. The only problem they have, he explains, is living space. But of course it is worse in Moscow.

'What do you do in Kiev?' asks the beauty, suddenly a little shy, I can see, in the presence of this cousin.

'I'm a mathematician,' he tells her.

The old man shakes his head.

'What, you make a living from arithmetic?'

'Not exactly. I work in a physics lab,' he replies.

And then he laughs, looking rather like a handsome wolf as he does so.

'There are stranger professions. Do you remember my brother Lev, the one with red hair? He is a poet. A Russian poet. A member of the Writers' Union. Though a year ago …'

He stops, and I guess at some recent problems.

'And this is a trade?' demands the old man.

'You get ration cards, a flat.'

'So why have you come back to the *stetl*, if everything is Paradise in Kiev?'

'Family is family. I wanted to warn you. I have heard rumours…'

'There are always rumours, ' says the old man.

The Kiev cousin stares at me, while they explain my relationship to the family.

And so begins the gossip about Menachem Mendl: his ability to memorise whatever he read seems to have been a legend. The newcomer is unimpressed by it. The Talmud. The Mishnah. The Gemara. No one wanted to learn that stuff any more.

'He was cleverer than all of you,' says the old man, who is probably the only one in the room who remembers him.

Now the beauty enters the conversation.

'He and his brothers went to England. Was that such a mistake?'

Yefraim mutters sullenly.

'It's no safer than here. Look what happened in Germany. The Jews thought they were at home there once.'

The beauty murmured, 'The Germans have wonderful music.'

'And for that is it worth losing a Jewish soul?' demands the old man. 'The Gypsies play their violins, too, and has it brought them happiness?'

She is not afraid of the old man, and he knows it, but he frowns at her. It is an argument they have had many times. He disagrees with all of them in different ways. He probably still reads the books Menachem Mendl loved. But he has endured a harder life and there are no laughter lines round his eyes.

'His children will go to university,' the Kiev cousin observes.

'A *Goyishe* university?' asks the old man.

'So? They learn the laws of science.'

'And can they grasp eternity, infinity, with all their science? A Jew without God can be persuaded of anything,' the old man sighs.

'They will learn the great literature of the world,' the beauty joins in.

This incenses the old man.

'All the writing of the world is filled with violence and fornication. Your *Anna Karenina, Madame Bovary* and our own Yiddish writers are all the same: once you worship art, you cannot worship God.'

'These are books you have read?' the Kiev cousin wonders, a little slyly.

'Long ago,' he assures him. 'When I was younger than you. And I tell you, even if we cannot carry our traditions into the next generation, while I am alive we shall stay here together. In Rechytsa.'

Then the whole family begin to speak at once: about France, that trollop of a country, and what it means that Stalin is Hitler's ally, with Poland split between Nazi Germany and Soviet Russia.

'Stalin knows what he's doing,' says the Kiev cousin.

The old man is sceptical.

'And what is he doing?'

'Building tanks, building planes …'

I want to cry out: 'Have you learned nothing? Leave. Leave now,' but I can hardly breathe in the hot, sticky air, let alone speak. And the solidity of the room is melting.

On the slopes of the underworld Der Nister rebukes me gently: *And where could they go? To live in Kiev will not make them safe.*

20 Golden Kiev

Here we are in the capital of old Rus:
with painted eggs, embroidered *rushniki*
and spicy Cossack dishes. This
is a city of ancient superstitions;
of tree spirits; of Bulgakov and Gogol.

Look at the Monastery of Golden Domes,
the teal blue of St Andrei's church.
Let's take the funicular into the Podol
– that beehive of gangsters and poetry –
but not that green line metro

to the edge of town, and the flat meadow
where eighty thousand Jews – doctors,
factory workers, children, mothers struggling –
were made to undress for German guns, then thrown
into Babiy Yar, to be smashed against the stones.

21 A Change in the Climate, 1953

Ehrenburg is sitting in a shabby chair in his Moscow flat with a blanket pulled up to his collar, smoking. On a small wooden table nearby stands a Dubonnet ashtray long ago stolen from a French café. This holds a row of stubbed cigarettes, as well as his favourite pipe. A bottle of wine stands next to it, but he is not drinking. Not talking much either. He coughs every time smoke enters his lungs.

Ehrenburg has not known a calm moment since January. Adrenalin courses through his blood, sending his heart out of rhythm. Now he refuses the coffee Lyubova has made for him. Her coconut cakes make him cough. He is sixty-two and frail, with an infection which returns every winter. He takes little notice of it.

Tsvetaeva shakes her head as she sees how little he looks after his health. Every sinew is visible in his neck.

And this is January, his birthday month. There has been an article in *Pravda* announcing the arrest of nine doctors; all with Jewish names, all said to be part of a Jewish conspiracy to poison leading Soviet figures. Zhdanov was said to be one of the victims. Would such rubbish be believed? There were many pure Russians who had reason to hate Zhdanov. And in any case, Zhdanov died of natural causes.

But yes, the people *did* believe the charges. In hospitals, patients cowered away from their doctors; Jewish medical students were sent off to remote areas of the country. First fear. Then hatred. Bewildered letters began to arrive from mothers with sons beaten up in school, or abused in the streets. Even as they asked for his help, they made it clear that they no longer trusted him.

This month, he is to receive the Stalin Peace Prize in the Kremlin's Sverdlov Hall. He knows the accusations. Survival always suggests complicity. He is already uneasy, thinking of it, before the arrival of an official he hardly knows, even before he is asked to condemn the imprisoned doctors in his speech. He makes clear that he would rather not collect his prize. The public relations disaster of such a refusal is evident and he is not pressed.

We watch him dress, coughing painfully as he bends to pull up his trousers, many times pausing for breath. Lyubova is dressed and ready.

And now we are following him along Little Borotitsky Hill on the north side of the Moskva. There is the Kremlin. A fortified city. Here, Ivan the Terrible arranged his own great Terror. Here Napoleon watched Moscow burn. As we enter, my eyes dazzle with golden boss and spandrel.

When Ehrenburg rises to thank Stalin for the honour he is receiving, he pays tribute to all those defamed, persecuted and enduring interrogation in prison. A chill goes round the hall. People hold their breath.

Tsvetaeva whispers: *Tomorrow, when the speech appears in 'Pravda', they will add a few words to make it seem he is talking about the West. Nothing is solved by gestures. And the story is far from over.*

At his dacha, in February, we watch him planting bulbs sent by the Queen of England – indoors, naturally: the snow has not yet melted, though there is a wintry sun. Lyubova nervously shows in two new visitors. Both are Jewish, both significant figures in the Party. They want him to sign an open letter to Stalin, *asking that the Jews be sent to Birobidzhan for their own protection against the wrath of the Russian people.* The legitimate wrath, they say. Carefully. They watch his face. He can see they are afraid.

His refusal is curt. When they have gone, he packs a suitcase for a return to Moscow.

Tsvetaeva tells me: *Dozens of other Jewish writers and musicians have also been approached. Not all have signed. A war hero and an opera singer refused.*

But only Ehrenburg has the impudence to write a letter to Stalin directly. Of course, he has no hope of changing Stalin's mind. He has been told of shacks already built for exiled Jews in Siberia, lists of Jews and their addresses drawn up in the major cities. Stalin is well prepared.

Nevertheless, he writes. It is a reckless letter, couched politely and loyally, but reminding Stalin of likely repercussions. His usual trick. He points out that a letter signed by a group of people united only by their Jewishness was likely to stir up the very nationalism Stalin wanted to discourage; that it would surely give ammunition to the enemies of the Soviet State abroad. He wrote as if puzzled what to do, needing advice from a wise leader. He knows it unlikely that Stalin will credit his submissive tone, since he would know of his earlier refusals.

Tsvetaeva sighs: *The original letter will be sent to newspapers with Ehrenburg's name attached to it anyway.*

His winter bronchitis returns, his phlegm is yellow-green and he begins to shiver even when the room is too hot.

Lyubova is unusually stalwart. She brings him tea with lemon, and lumps of sugar. They wait to see what will happen next.

What happens is that Stalin suffers a cerebral haemorrhage on 5 March and dies. There are frenzied tears, panic, people trampled to death in Red Square.

Ehrenburg finds it impossible to feel the appropriate relief. Who can predict what will happen under new leaders in this blood-soaked country? He has seen too much death and cruelty. Sitting in his chair, trying to recover, still coughing badly, he remembers Ukrainians and Lithuanians collaborating with Hitler's murderous troops. All his life he had fought the Fascism of Hitler and the Germans, only to find it flourishing in his own motherland.

As March goes on, the ice floes begin to melt in the Moskva but the streets are like glass after dark and the darkness comes early. The doctors are released. But there are no visitors, and few phone calls, even from people who know him well. It is as if the whole population has been stunned, and can only cope by remaining inside their own flats silently.

Sitting in his chair, with his fever rising over 100 degrees every evening, Ehrenburg's memories go back painfully over the years. Most of the time, he is on the edge of weeping. He and Lyubova only returned to Russia when the German troops took Paris. They had to find shelter in the Soviet Embassy, a refuge possible only because Stalin was Hitler's ally. As Soviet citizens, they could travel back through Berlin, staying in a hotel clearly marked 'For Aryans Only'. Lyubova saw the notice, but she was more terrified of returning to Russia, and had to be carried on to the train.

How did he learn that Isaac Babel had been murdered? And when? He must have guessed as much during the war.

Or just afterwards, looking through the ruins of Kiev, close by the deathly ravine of Babiy Yar where so many died. Of course he knew. He gave money to Babel's second wife when most people were afraid to meet her. But after the war, when he met the first wife in France, why had he told her Babel was still alive?

What was it possible to feel when the Russian armies took Berlin? Elation? Relief? Hatred? He remembers writing in a poem that he waited for victory as a man waits for a woman he loves, and could not recognise her when she arrived.

At night, while Lyubova sleeps, he sits up in the half-light of a single bulb and is reminded how he and Vasilii Grossman put together letters and interviews with Jewish survivors of the German massacres: *The Black Book of Soviet Jewry*. At first, it even seemed the book might be published. But, suddenly, it was forbidden to distinguish Jewish suffering from that of the Soviet people as a whole. There were reasons. One was the newly formed State of Israel, which Stalin had supported with the other members of the Security Council, but always suspected.

When Golda Meir arrived in Moscow, the enthusiasm of the local Jews was unguarded. Ehrenburg shakes his head at the memory but he cannot help admiring their lack of caution. After the Warsaw Ghetto, the rising of Sobibor, after the murders at Auschwitz and Maidanek, how can it not seem miraculous that a group of Jews fought off so many Arab armies? They called out the traditional Passover greeting to Meir: 'Next Year in Jerusalem'. They stood in the streets to have a sight of the delegation, and some had tears in their eyes. Ehrenburg kept a little distance. He had never been a Zionist; his hope was assimilation, not separation.

The moment he heard that Mikhoels has been killed in a traffic accident in Minsk, Ehrenburg knew it was an assassination. It was 1948. Mikhoels had been sent to Minsk as a member of the Stalin Prize committee, supposedly to review a play. He and another critic were called away from their hotel. Both bodies were found early the next morning. A truck had run over both of them.

That was when Ehrenburg began to understand. That winter, the Kremlin arrested twenty-five new defendants. All were secretly executed on 12 August 1952: 'The Night of the Murdered Poets'. Ehrenburg thinks with discomfort, as he often has: 'I am the only one of the Jewish Anti-Fascist Committee still alive.'

The only survivor.

Well, now he has survived Stalin. With that thought, his temperature falls to normal. Spring comes fully, the rivers of Moscow glint in the sunshine and he begins to write again. A new novel: *The Thaw*.

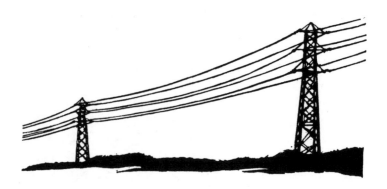

22 The fortunate spirit

In a brief downpour of summer rain, we are
staring through Pasternak's windows together.
Overhead, there is a sudden peal of thunder.

'Look at the lamplight falling over his papers,
how easily the ink glides over the vellum.
He will be happy,' Tsvetaeva murmurs,

'as a writer is happy, surprised by his own images.
He and a new love will breathe happily
until she is taken off to the camps as a hostage.

His novel will grow in a warm and well-lit room,
while he imagines gusts of storm in the taiga,
and blames himself for what he did not suffer.'

23 Prizes

We stand at a little distance.

It is early October 1958. A freakish autumn. The trees have only just begun to lose their leaves. Red or translucent yellow, they float through the warm air; cover the grass, sit in the bushes.

At his kitchen window, Pasternak stares out at a single red bud on the winter rose tree. He is thinking about his meeting with Akhmatova, who, without saying an unkind word, makes clear her disapproval of his sending *Dr Zhivago* to be published in Italy. And not because she thinks it is dangerous but because she senses in him an eagerness for worldly acclaim, a passion she abandoned years ago and now despises. He does not defend himself.

For a last time, he murmurs how glad it would make him if she received his mistress, Olga Ivinskaya, now returned from the camps, but Akhmatova remains unwilling to do so. He does not press her to explain that reluctance. Nothing to do with his wife, he is certain. Some rumour, perhaps. There are so many. And he frowns as he remembers some of Olga's own stories. She told him he was always called 'the old Jew' by her interrogators, that they insisted it was impossible for a young Russian beauty to love a Jew.

Someone enters the room and he knows without turning round that it is Zinaida. He can hear her bustling about, attending to this chore or that. She, too, is angry with him, because of his foolishness in sending the novel abroad. She knows little of the literary world, but shakes her head when he tries to reassure her that he has chosen a Communist publisher. He does not argue with her.

Pasternak has been writing the same novel for nine years, sometimes with the hope of publication in Soviet magazines. Why should he not hope for publication now? Not so very long ago he signed a contract with a journal for the first part of *Zhivago*. The worst times are over. There is no more talk of rootless cosmopolitans. *Noviy Mir* has published the first part of Ehrenburg's *The Thaw*. Poems of Tsvetaeva – and Ehrenburg's essay praising them – have appeared in Moscow journals.

But that was before the revolts in Hungary and Poland. Now, liberalisation no longer looks such a good idea. That is why Pasternak shows his manuscript to D'Angelo of Feltrinelli. He knows it is risky, which is why he tells D'Angelo, laughing: 'You are hereby invited to watch me face a firing squad.'

Olga is alarmed when he tells her D'Angelo took the manuscript away with him. Unlike Zinaida, she is, however, resourceful. She can negotiate with those in power, suggest compromises, wangle concessions. He is glad to have her act for him. 'Negotiations are a game of *bluff*,' he tells her, and smiles, as if he were optimistic about the outcome. All spring and summer the manuscript has been with Goslitizdat, after all. His poems are being published, and have been treated as important. He has even begun to write new poems.

Sometime in August, however, Ehrenburg visits him. He has spoken up publicly for the novel, but he tells Pasternak in private what he does not like. He disapproves of Pasternak's enthusiasm for the Orthodox Church. He is offended by the way he writes about Jews. His candour is scalding. He uses harsher words than Akhmatova has done.

Pasternak shows the novel to several younger writers, including Yevgeny Yevtushenko, who comes respectfully to the dacha to return it.

Yevtushenko is twenty-seven, dressed in slim jeans; his eyes are ice-blue. He puts the parcel he is carrying on the table, and stares into Pasternak's calm face. He has dealt with members of the KGB, met Khrushchev and has read his poems to stadiums of admirers. Nothing frightens him. But now he is agitated. He has brought a bottle of the best Georgian wine. Pasternak receives it with approval, pulls the cork, and brings glasses.

'You know I love your poems,' Yevtushenko begins. 'I have them by heart. And I am honoured that you trust me with your manuscript ... but –'

Pasternak smiles.

'You do not like the novel,' he observes equably.

'There are passages of great beauty. Of course. But what you say about the Civil War... you question the very foundation of the Soviet State.'

Pasternak voices no denial. His face remains impassive. He pours them both another glass of Georgian wine, retrieves the copy of *Zhivago*, and they talk of other matters.

When a few poems from the novel come out in an émigré Munich magazine, and the Italians advertise the forthcoming novel, Pasternak is asked to send a telegram halting publication. Zinaida cannot imagine what insanity makes him hesitate. Yet hesitate he does. Only when he hears from D'Angelo that no telegram will influence him does Pasternak send the instructions the authorities require. It is too late, as he knows it would be. Fury breaks around him in waves. He is told the novel will *never* be published in the Soviet Union.

But the Writers' Union has made a huge miscalculation there. The news of a ban – which soon leaks out – guarantees the interest of the world press, and huge sales. Suddenly, there are French, Dutch, English and German translations. Akhmatova shrugs and smiles when they meet. 'You will find Fame and Scandal are much the same,' she tells him sadly. She is remembering Zhdanov's decree in 1949, which took away her livelihood and deprived her of any chance of publication.

And then Ehrenburg brings other rumours. He has heard them from Louis Aragon, and he repeats them to Pasternak with anxiety rather than congratulations. It seems there is a good chance he will be offered the Nobel Prize, perhaps with another Russian writer. Perhaps alone. Pasternak had been nominated for the Nobel before, but now, even as he stands looking into the garden, he knows that the Prize will be no source of pride in Russia. The Writers' Union will take the decision of the Nobel Committee as a political insult. Too much has been written about Pasternak's heroism in the West.

Ehrenburg agrees it could be a disaster. Before he leaves, he has one suggestion to offer. Pasternak might approach the Writers' Union and propose they publish some safe part of *Zhivago* in Russia. That would defuse the excitement in the West. Pasternak considers the possibility. The two men sit together, drinking, as the light goes and the wind gets up. By evening, it has begun to rain heavily. There is a pile of leaves gathered together from the path to the house, their decay hastened by the rain. Pasternak watches Ehrenburg's frail figure disappearing into the watery night. The telegram arrives the next morning.

The citation is for his lyric poetry only, and for a moment Pasternak's face shows naked joy. Without thought, without shame, he sends back his acceptance: 'Immensely thankful, touched, proud, astonished, abashed.'

He knows what must follow.

Four days later, Pasternak is expelled from the Writers' Union. This takes away his right to the dacha in Peredelkino and any chance of literary earnings. Olga will cope, but Zinaida will be penniless. What else did he imagine? He has destroyed Zinaida's life, and his son's too, he reflects. Already, he repents of his hasty response.

He cannot sleep. The telephone is silent. The days pass in a single blank. Then, on 29 October, maddened by insomnia and Zinaida's tears, hardly able to breathe, Pasternak sends another telegram to refuse the prize. His gesture heals nothing. It is well known that only three laureates have ever declined an award, all of them in Hitler's Germany at the instructions of Hitler's government. Those at the centre of the Writers' Union are even more incensed and they propose a graver sentence: Pasternak will be deported, and deprived of Soviet citizenship.

Exile. His greatest dread.

Like Akhmatova, who had often been urged to leave Russia when it was still possible, Pasternak has always refused to live abroad. And for the same reason: a poet cannot leave his language. Life might be more comfortable with his family in Oxford, but he knows it would be more trivial. Now there is no choice.

The warmth has gone out of October altogether. Even with a huge log fire, Pasternak is shivering. He speaks to both Zinaida and Olga. Neither wants to leave Russia with him; there are children who cannot be abandoned. He begins to think death would be preferable to exile alone.

Suddenly, he cannot imagine why the Nobel Prize had ever seemed important to him. He is embarrassed by his telegram of acceptance. It was not a betrayal of Russia but of himself. He is ashamed of the words he had chosen, and his reckless speed in sending them.

We watch him walk around the rooms of his house in a fever. He cannot bring himself to telephone anyone. He cannot settle in a chair.

But he has not been forgotten by his friends. A draft is being composed, in part by Olga – who has received hints from Soviet authorities about what would play best – and in part by Ariadne Efron, Tsvetaeva's daughter, now returned from the Gulag. They cobble together a letter to be sent to Khrushchev.

Pasternak glances at it briefly and signs without fuss. He does not see it as capitulation. It is simply not important. No more than the Nobel Prize is important. All that matters is to stay in Russia and to write poems.

As November comes, with snow piled high against the tree trunks, he is not unhappy. The sun glitters on the ice. He pads over the snow to call on a friend, breathing sleety air into his bronchitic lungs without complaint. He has lived a charmed life, he reflects. Why has God been so kind to him? He cannot understand it, as he remembers so many less fortunate. Mandelstam. Tsvetaeva. And a list of others. 'I am not worthy,' he often mutters. He rarely sees Akhmatova these days.

His hero Doctor Zhivago travels at the end of his book towards the Botkin Hospital where Pasternak spent three months after a heart attack a few years earlier. Zhivago never reaches it.

Pasternak thinks no more of suicide. Death will come soon enough.

24 Joseph

Europe below us, water and stone,
falling like Venice into the sea. A young
man with ginger hair stands alone,

on Pushkin's parapet, with shoulders
like a footballer, his forehead slant.
'What are the things you remember,

Joseph?' Tsvetaeva whispers tenderly.
'Your words, Marina.' 'But from your own life?'
'Just now I thought of sliding happily

over the snow to school as a little boy,
my head already filled with Russian poetry,
my fists ready for a playground battle.

When did I first learn I was Jewish scum?
It was long before my wife
refused the name of Brodsky to my son.

Well, in America, my new homeland,
my books, my bed sheets, and an unchained door
bewildered those who could not understand

I only cared for poetry and talk.
So I was rude, almost a boor; perhaps
that's why they liked me in New York.

Here, with only a candle for company, I wonder
how it was I took their honours as easily
as I picked Chinese dumplings from a trolley.'

25 Arkangelskoye 1964

It is a White Night in the far north, an evening with the sun
yellow on the horizon, and a strange euphoric light which
bleaches the firs and marshes.

An old train, with its windows barred and boarded up,
its compartments packed, is transporting prisoners from the
Kresty Prison in Leningrad to the far north. It stops at
Konusha, a station in the southern sector of the Arkangelsk
region, and a group of exiles – including a red-haired young
man with a high forehead and powerful shoulders – are
taken out unceremoniously.

The young man is Joseph Brodsky.

The village has no more than fourteen huts, all of them in
pale wood. People who live there work on a State farm,
their tractors scraping off topsoil which rests on granite. The
land is being ruined by the new methods of farming.

Brodsky is taken to a hut at the very edge of this cluster
of houses.

He has been sentenced to five years hard labour but he
is used to manual work. He left school at fifteen and worked
in a factory and a morgue before hauling instruments for
geological expeditions in the far north. Half taiga. Half
tundra. These jobs were his university. He is prepared for
vodka made out of wood alcohol; an empty store which sells
only loaves of bread and cans of foul-tasting fish. He makes
friends with his neighbours, though at first they are
suspicious of him.

And what does he remember now of Leningrad? The ceilings in the great houses collapsed. Their windows shattered. Inside, furniture and books burned for warmth. Between the shrapnel-pitted walls and the grey-green façades, the streets are empty.

To him, Leningrad is the most beautiful city in the world. His family lived in a room and a half between Nevsky Prospekt and Liteiny Prospekt, not far from the palaces, colonnades and pilasters of the centre. The iron bridges over the canals, the huge stretches of water going out to sea, suggest an infinite world elsewhere. All of it belongs to him.

Money has been short since his father was sacked from the navy when Zhdanov decreed no Jew could hold the rank of Major. Joseph has to answer that crucial fifth question in all his registration papers as 'Jewish', but he takes no account of it. He is not so much a rebel, as wilfully irresponsible. He walks out of school, teaches himself what he wants to know – even plans to hijack a plane across the border into Afghanistan. But his most important act is to write poetry. By twenty-one he has been published in *samizdat* all over Russia. Akhmatova praises him, even dedicates a poem to him. The KGB have already taken him into prison twice. His friends suggest he would be safer in Moscow. He tries it for a time, but returns when he hears his girlfriend has taken up with another man.

One very cold night in Leningrad, he is walking along a street when three men surround him and ask for his name. When he refuses to go along with them, they bring up a car, twist his arms behind his back and take him to the Kresty prison.

Here in the north, he does not often think about his trial, held on 18 February 1964 in the District Courts on Vosstanie Street. Or the huge crowd of young people moving along a dark and dirty corridor trying to enter the room where his trial is to be held.

The judge, a stout, morose woman of about forty, mutters with some surprise: 'I did not expect such a crowd.'

Somebody responds: 'It is not so common these days to try a poet.'

She shrugs. Inside there are very few friends of Brodsky's. Permission to be a spectator is stringently restricted. The only literary notables present are those like Admoni and Etkind who are brave enough to be speaking for the defence. And Frida Vigdarova, who takes notes.

In the dock, Brodsky manages an enfeebled wave to his parents. He is twenty-four.

The judge frowns. To be a social parasite is a serious charge.

'What is your profession?' she asks him.

'Writing poetry. Translation,' he replies.

'Why didn't you find work?'

'I did work. I wrote poetry.'

'What institution are you connected with?'

'None. I made contracts with publishers.'

'What are these contracts, and how much are they for?'

'I can't remember exactly. My lawyers have the documents.'

The judge is clearly exasperated.

'What is your specialist qualification?'

'Poet. Poet translator.'

'But who declared you to be a poet? Who put you on the list of poets?'

'No one. Who put me on the list of human beings?'

A little buzz goes round the court, which is quickly stilled.
'And did you study for this?'
'For what?'
'For being a poet. Did you take a course in higher education?'
'I don't think it comes from education.'
'Where does it come from, then? Poetry?'
'I think it comes from – God.'

It is an answer that will go round Russia, and inevitably reach the West. He is already famous before the judge delivers her sentence. He is remanded to an asylum for psychiatric investigation, to be brought back for a further trial.

'Have you any questions?'
'I have a request. I should like to have a pen and paper in my cell.'

═══════

But he does not want to be famous as a victim.

In hospital with flu, he dreams of Ossia, his fluffy, ash-grey cat with eyes green as gooseberries. He adores cats: imperturbable, elegant creatures who don't make a single movement without grace. And he remembers the bridges over the Neva, the Moika canal and an icy courtyard filled with snow in the industrial outskirts of Leningrad.

When his friends Yevgeny Rein and Anatoly Naiman – also poet protégés of Akhmatova – come to visit him in Arkangelskoye, they find he has made himself at home in his hut. His good spirits astonish them. He tells them he is not much bothered by his sentence, that he is writing well (as he is) and has a radio he can tune to the BBC. He makes light of the work, the cold, the suppers of cabbage mash, the absence of women. At fifteen, he was working as a milling machine operator. He is used to hard work.

As he drinks, he answers their questions without allowing them to pity him: 'You get up at six in the morning. Go out in the rain or snow or summer heat. There's no phone. No people to talk to. No women. But it's okay.'

When Rein asks about his time in the Kresty, he answers: 'Prison is not so bad. Not enough space. Too much time.'

He does not want sympathy.

He describes the Kresty Prison: the Piranesi galleries, the walls of his cell which were brick but smeared with green oil paint, a barred window closed to the outside world. He does not minimise the horrors of the psychiatric clinic where the judge sent him first: the iron soldiers' cots, too close together, the violent men injected with sulphur. And the Wrap: inmates forced into icy baths, wrapped in wet sheets, put next to a radiator so that the sheets would dry out and, in doing so, tear off skin.

But his serenity is unforced. He tells them: 'I thank God I am a stranger. And that I have no homeland.'

He shrugs away memories of his wife, who is tall, with soft features and brown hair down to her shoulders. She speaks little and smiles like the Mona Lisa. Some time after his friends visit she decides to join him in the far north, and

111

he is glad. But something is broken between them. Not just because she went off with his friend Dmitri Bobyshev that New Year's Eve when he was hiding in Moscow. She finds him too intense. He remembers his father saying of her, 'She has dilute milk instead of blood in her veins.'

When his friends have gone, the solitude around him is as palpable as the Arctic cold. He tells himself: 'I belong to the Russian language. I am still a Russian poet.'

26 Farewell

Marina has become Eurydice.
She cries out, even as she vanishes:
'I am nowhere. Do not look for me.

Alive, I was always a bewildered creature,
a night bird blinded with light, a stranger
whose ordinary world was ash and sand.'

'Have you led me here to abandon me?'
I call out. Silence. I am alone at the edge
of a black river, with snow in the harsh air,

until a voice begins in my ear: 'Be calm.
Are you not tempted to give up and sleep?
There are those ready to hold you in their arms.

Soon everyone must enter the realm of night.
Give up then, as Marina did. Why fight?'
And now I see the presence at my side:

androgyne, with smooth dog skin and wild
blue eyes. He pads along with me – not
that good Devil Marina met as a child,

in her sister's room with secret patchouli
inks and oils, and dangerous silver pills –
not sexual life, but Death sent up to tempt me.

I pull away, as soon as I have named him,
and plunge my bare soul into the freezing waters;
there, gasping, obstinate, wanting to live: I swim.

27 St Petersburg 2005

It is raining heavily. Daylight has gone, and the dazzling shop windows streak the wet streets with colour. Along Nevsky Prospekt the traffic bunches up: coveted Mercedes in metallic silver paint press close to old Soviet bangers, all churning the rain water with their tyres, equally trapped. The cars move in jerks, at little more than five miles an hour. No sense in hoping for a lift home.

Where the gutters are clogged, water floods the pavement. Everything is a blur of shiny black asphalt and headlights. I check the names of the shabby streets I am passing as I walk away from the Neva. A particular café is my marker. Azerbaijani or Uzbek. Close by a bookshop where they sell CDs, as I remember it.

At the Moika, a sign warns me that the water is rising dangerously.

My raincoat is not fully waterproof and, as I approach Sadovaya, the clammy wool beneath is uncomfortable. I am shivering, but at least I know where I am. Soon I am making my way under a yellow stucco arch into a familiar courtyard. I tread carefully, looking for potholes. My ankles are weak, my balance unreliable. In the far corner I can see my rented flat. Home. For a moment I fumble anxiously for the keys in my pocket and sigh with relief to find the whole necessary bunch of them.

Can I remember the sequence in which they must be unlocked? I can.

Once inside, the heat of the flat envelops me like a

blessing. I pull off all my wet clothes, and throw myself into the bed, exhausted, falling asleep almost immediately.

When I wake, I know I have been ill. As I put my feet to the floor, my legs are still shaky. But my appetite astonishes me. Slipping on a dressing gown, I go to the kitchen. There are matches, and a bottle of water. Hot tea restores my spirit.

In the refrigerator, I find six eggs, butter and half a loaf of bread which is stale but could be toasted. And as I eat the scrambled eggs eagerly, wondering how long I have been asleep, my dreams begin to fade and in their place rise memories.

It was certainly the hand of Tsvetaeva that brought me to Moscow in 1975, though the invitation came through Yevgeny Yevtushenko. I had already translated a book of her poems, and went round the house with her voice in my head. I was working on her biography, but I had not yet planned my first visit to the Soviet Union.

Yevtushenko himself was in any case her gift to me. He made a habit of including some of her poems at his readings on a tour of the States, using whatever English translation he could find. He knew my name only because my version of 'Attempt at Jealousy' seemed to please his audiences. At dinner with George Steiner in Churchill College, he was astonished to discover I lived in Cambridge. He came round that very evening, with his wife Jan, and stayed until it was light, drinking and talking in our green room hanging above the river about his admiration for Tsvetaeva.

When I first visited Moscow, under Brezhnev, I flew into Russia over Latvia. The rivers were frozen, though the roads were clear. Green shadows of trees seemed to move over the white fields between the villages. The plane landed on a clear runway though the snow was falling and there were piles of frozen slush taller than a man. Zhenya Yevtushenko met me with a gift of red carnations. He was in a green velvet suit with a velvet peaked cap, his face young then, his eyes a brilliant Siberian blue. It was his heyday. His arrival at my hotel provoked a flurry of visible excitement among the receptionists. To walk with him in the streets of Moscow was like walking with a Beatle at the time of *Sergeant Pepper's Lonely Hearts Club Band*.

I was in Moscow to gather material for my biography of Tsvetaeva. That evening, my friend Masha Enzensberger came to collect me from the hotel to have supper with her mother, the poet Margarita Aliger; Aliger was part of the commission set up to promote Tsvetaeva's memory, which had included both Marina's daughter Alya and Ilya Ehrenburg , until he died in 1967. Alya herself had died of a heart attack only a few weeks before I arrived in Moscow.

We walked in the burning cold across Red Square towards St Basil's, then over a bridge of the Moskva to Lavrushinsky, the distinguished writers' house where both Pasternak and Ehrenburg had lived in their time, and where Aliger now had a spacious apartment.

She was a small, brown-eyed woman in her sixties with sadness in her face. Her sitting room was crammed with heavy furniture, her sideboard covered with ornaments. The table was spread with a Madeira tablecloth and on that cloth she had set out black bread with olives, slices of onion, smoked fish and salt fish, marrow and aubergines with slivers of garlic. Sour cucumbers were pickled in garlic and brine rather than sweet dill, and their very smell evoked my childhood home. Polish Jews favour a sour-sweet cucumber; indeed that sweetness marks off Polish-Jewish from Russian-Jewish cuisine.

Aliger herself had led a dramatic life, though her early years began happily enough. Her Jewish family in Odessa supported the Revolution; her mother read Russian poetry to her. Her father played the violin and composed a little music. The new regime offered Aliger the chance to study chemistry and then literature in Moscow, and her first poems were published when she was little more than a schoolgirl.

Her face in early photographs is alert and eager, a little like that of Anne Frank, with large eyes and a rather pointed nose; the face the celebrated novelist Alexander Fadeev must have known when they were lovers during the Second World War. He was a powerful man, then General Secretary of the Writers' Union. He had a tough-boned face, with a cleft chin. A guerrilla fighter in two wars, his courage showed in merciless eyes. In contrast, Aliger's expression was tremulous. They never married (Fadeev already had a wife) but Aliger's only surviving child is his.

By the time I met her in her sixties, her shoulders had begun to stoop. The loss of those she loved had marked her whole life. Her first husband, Konstantin Mazakov-Rakitin, was a composer. Their first child died of meningitis at eight months. At the outbreak of the Second World War, while her husband went to the Front, she travelled to the frozen wastes of Christopol in the Tatar republic, sharing a carriage with Akhmatova and Pasternak, and observing their composure with reverence. Perhaps she learned from their preternatural calm how to bear the loss of her own husband early in the war.

Small-boned and delicate, she flew into Leningrad at the

height of the siege and joined Olga Berggoltz and Vera Inber in broadcasts to encourage the trapped citizens there. The guns were never silent. She saw the emaciated bodies of those who dropped and froze to death in the snow. She saw old people dragged away on sledges, and others left where they fell.

During the last years of Fadeev's life, they were estranged. He began to drink heavily, and in 1956 he killed himself. For many years people attributed his death to a moment of drunken depression, but the date of his death is significant. In 1956, Khrushchev exposed the murderous extent of Stalin's madness, and Fadeev was in despair at his own complicity. Masha told me stories of writers saved by him, but there can be no doubt about the role he played in the terrible fate of others. Many of Aliger's lyrics turn on the unhappiness of being a survivor.

And Fadeev was not her last loss. Her elder daughter died of tuberculosis a few years before my visit to Moscow. Masha was now her only child. And I could see there was some tension between them. She often felt guilt mixed with anger and a poignant sense of the irreparable. And these emotions found their way into one of her best short lyrics:

Once again they've quarrelled on a tram,
    shamelessly indifferent to strangers.
I can't hide how much I envy them.
    I can't take my eyes off their behaviour.

They don't even know their good fortune,
    and not knowing is part of their luck.
Think of it. They are together. Alive.
    And have the time to sort things out and make up.

Aliger had arranged for me to meet a number of Tsvetaeva's friends. Among them was Viktoria Schweitzer, who had long been writing her own biography of Tsvetaeva, and Pavel Antokolsky, whom Marina had been in love with during the Civil War years.

When Tsvetaeva knew him, Antokolsky was a small, curly-haired boy wearing a student's jacket; a talented poet of seventeen, learning to be a playwright. His twinkly charm, enormous eyes and huge voice when he spoke his poetry out loud, earned him the nickname of Pushkin. At the time he was closest to Tsvetaeva, he was also in the middle of a homosexual love affair with Yuri Zavadsky, an actor at the same theatre. Tsvetaeva fell in love with both men, and both remained her friends.

I could see Antokolsky had once been handsome, though the lids of his eyes were maroon and there were heavy pouches under them. Now in his seventies, he resembled a *New Yorker* cartoon of a fashionable roué. His hair and long moustache were carefully combed, and he wore a velvet jacket. He said very little, however, and when he spoke his voice seemed to come through some impediment in the throat.

I sensed something evasive in him. Perhaps he felt guilty because he had failed to help Tsvetaeva when she came to Moscow in 1941, desperate for friendship. He wanted to explain to me how it was then, how she seemed to be an altogether different woman, alienated from the people around her.

'*Elle est autre,*' he said several times.

In contrast, Viktoria Schweitzer was a large, forthright woman, who would have been suspicious of me if she had not been assured I was a poet. I already knew a great deal about Tsvetaeva herself, but all that I knew of her husband

Sergei Efron's story had been told to me by Vera Traill. One of Vera's wildest tales – as I thought – had Efron recruiting her as a member of an NKVD cell. She spoke of his involvement in the murder of Ignace Reiss, the Soviet defector.

I was hesitant to repeat the story, because Efron, in everyone's account, was a gentle, indecisive figure and an unlikely hitman. But there were many anomalies in his allegiance. He had been a half-Jew fighting in the White Army even though his parents were revolutionaries. I knew that he had been brought back to the Soviet Union soon after the murder, that Tsvetaeva had been interrogated by the French police.

Viktoria Schweitzer leaned across the table to pick up a pickled tomato before she replied vehemently:

'It is all true.'

'But why?' I wanted to know, stupidly.

'In those terrible years,' she shrugged. 'He wanted to return to Russia; he was told he must show his obedience. I suppose he did what he was told. And when the French police moved in on him, he was taken off back to Russia. They rewarded him with a house in Bolshevo.'

Aliger, I remember, added quietly: 'Let's not talk about taking the wrong road. What was the right road? You think back along the way for signs – was it this way, that decision, this thin tree, this signpost? He wanted to return to Russia. It was the price.'

When I knew her better, she told me, 'People do not forgive me my mistakes.' She was thinking of her unquestioning Communist allegiance, I suppose, but her domestic behaviour had also been damaging. I was very sympathetic to Aliger, who had lost a daughter and a first husband, and had probably never been as important a presence in Fadeev's life as he was in hers. But Masha, I knew, found her bossy and unjust, someone who did not recognise her daughter's successes, and belittled her even without intending to do so. She refused to be defined as Aliger's daughter, even though her own privileged life came entirely from Aliger's importance in the *nomenklatura*.

This I grasped for the first time when Aliger took me for lunch at the Writers' Club. Dom Literaterov was once the magnificent house Tolstoy describes as belonging to the Rostov family in *War and Peace*. Though there were no gracious ladies now to be seen, and no Natasha to lean elegantly out of a window into the moonlight, the privileges to which the card of a writer gave access when the Soviet Union was still a great power were immense. It was an exclusive club where writers could arrange their holidays, their dachas, their publication. And Aliger, who seemed so unassuming and whose work had not yet reached the West, caused space to clear around us as we approached. We were given the table of her choice.

There were enormous chandeliers. Oak walls. Alcoves. White cloths on the tables. Pewter dishes shaped like little saucepans in which chicken livers were served with mushrooms and walnuts. There was a long table of sturgeon, radishes, fresh cucumbers, red salmon eggs, black and gleaming caviar. The Moscow Writers' Club had the best chef in Moscow.

We were joined by Yunna Moritz, a distinguished poet of the generation younger than Aliger. She had a long, pale face, sad grey eyes and, on this first meeting at least, a gentle voice. Moritz had been a great favourite of Akhmatova. Later, I discovered she also had something of Akhmatova's pride, the same majesty. She introduced herself to me with the sentence, 'I am a very strange poet.' Then we talked freely, and sadly, of the matchless genius of Russian women poets, their authority, their confidence, and their tragic fate.

Moritz was born in 1937 in Kiev, of Jewish parentage, and as we sat round the white table, with waiters fussing about us, it occurred to me for the first time that we were all Jewish people, and that perhaps this connection – for all its historical dangers – could be a bond in the Soviet Union.

I knew so little then.

Two decades later, in the buzz of a failed military coup, I sat in the same restaurant with Aliger and Moritz, and listened to their stories. For all the street victory, the times were no longer euphoric. A section of the Writers' Union proclaimed the anti-Semitic ideals of the Black Hundreds; both women had been sent abusive letters. Neither had much faith in Yeltsin's wish to control the Mafia, and certainly none in his power to do so. Their voices were muted, uneasy.

There was no regret for Gorbachov, however. *Glasnost* had depleted their incomes, since the Russian people now lusted after pornography from the West. The following day, Yunna was going to Perm to give a reading, and she told me there would only be a small audience. Less than four thousand, she thought. I had to ask her to repeat the figure. When she came to read at the Cambridge Poetry Festival, I reminded her, we were proud to muster four hundred. But what happened in Great Britain no longer mattered to her. Only the United States could offer her what she needed. She planned to travel to a university there next spring and to supplement her Moscow earnings with a term's teaching.

She was a warm, ebullient, powerful woman whose world had collapsed.

I am lucky, she conveyed to me. There are people more trapped than I am.

And Aliger was among those too frail to make such a journey. A sorrowful brown bird, she seemed to me, though I knew she had unexpectedly made a late marriage to a younger man in the last year. Not long after my return to London, a few weeks after she heard of her daughter's death from an overdose of sleeping pills, she died of a heart attack in the street.

Yunna Moritz, on the other hand, became more and more imperious as her life became difficult. Some time in 1998, while I was writing a life of Pushkin, I visited her at home in Moscow. She sent her husband to collect me from a Metro station and bring me to her flat. He was her third husband, I think; a calm, patient man who must have needed all his gentleness to cope with Yunna.

I was wearing the amber necklace – which looked like a string of yellowing animal teeth – that she had given me on a visit to Cambridge. She said it would protect me. And there was a period in the 1980s when I wore it every day, superstitiously, as Tsvetaeva might have done, even to collect the post. I told her as much, but she was not amused by my story.

Indeed, I began to be aware of a banked-up fury underneath the warmth of her welcome. She was angry with me because I knew so little about what was going on in Moscow that year. The anarchy. The brutality. The way murder for a few roubles had become commonplace. Corpses were left for days untended on the subways. The week before, her son had been taken into hospital with a head wound and she had been unable to find him for three days.

Her flat was small and she did not want to talk about Pushkin. Everyone talked about Pushkin, she told me crossly. And his courage. Was it so brave to tell the Tsar he would have been part of the Decembrist revolt if he had been in St Petersburg? It was no more than a clever stratagem. Rather than Pushkin, she honoured Ryleev, who had actually *been* on Senate Square and was afterwards executed in a horribly bungled hanging. A fine poet and a genuine liberal, she insisted.

She came close to accusing Pushkin of tacit collaboration with Nicholas, though she backed off from calling him a *trimmer*. I did not argue strenuously. I could not help feeling that she was talking about herself, and the contrast between her own fortune and those of other poets who were now coming into prominence. She shrugged off the names I mentioned, and showed little admiration for any, even her own contemporaries like Bella Akhmadulina. An era had ended, and she was not optimistic about what was likely to come next.

To me, she seemed indomitable. And, for all her pessimism, she continues to write and publish. As I left, she gave me her latest book: children's poems with her own illustrations. I gave her mine, though I doubted she would read it in English.

Writers' gifts.

28 Pasternak's Grave

Some time in the winter of 1978, I was taken by Yevtushenko to see Pasternak's grave in Peredelkino.

We left the car near the Pasternak dacha, a two-storied wooden building, not yet a museum. One of the rooms on the upper floor was lit, but this was a spontaneous visit after a Moscow party and there was no question of disturbing whoever was living there. We walked across a field to the Writers' Cemetery.

The great poet's profile in bas-relief on the gravestone was peaceful and grand. I remember a dark blue sky and a light scattering of snow on the ground. Birch trees lay behind the gravestones and there was an unlit candle at the foot of the grassy mound.

'Seventy years old,' Yevtushenko said, more to himself than to me. 'An amazing age for a Russian poet.'

On this visit, my husband was travelling with me. While I was taken in Aliger's chauffeur-driven car to look at the place where Tsvetaeva's childhood house had once stood on Three Ponds Lane, and the flat she and Seryozha had lived in at the corner of Boris and Gleb when they were first married, my husband visited the distinguished immunologist Raoul Nezlin, the son (I later discovered) of one of the Jewish doctors imprisoned by Stalin at the time of the 'Doctors' Plot'.

Nezlin was in some minor trouble himself in 1978, and

had been denied foreign visitors. An interesting deal was struck, whereby my husband visited a friend of Nezlin's in the same laboratory, evidently not so restricted, in return for chemicals which were hard to obtain but available to Nezlin.

For supper we went together to that friend's flat, which I was astonished to discover was much smaller and far less well furnished than Aliger's. Poets were evidently accorded a higher status than most scientists. He seemed to find that unsurprising, and spoke of Aliger with great respect. When I mentioned I was meeting Yevtushenko the following day, however, he could not conceal his hostility. He was, we had already discovered, also Jewish, and I thought he ought at the very least to be grateful for Yevtushenko's courage in recalling the massacre of Jews at Babiy Yar.

He agreed. But that was then, and now, he managed to convey, Yevtushenko was no more than a tool of the regime.

Suspicions of Yevtushenko were not yet commonplace in the West, though there was always some astonishment that he was allowed to travel so freely when other writers had trouble with visas. He was, of course, an unashamed advocate of Socialism – of Lenin rather than Stalin, he was at pains to point out – and I assumed his charm and enthusiasm were explanation enough for the licence accorded to him. He enjoyed some of the same privileges accorded to Ilya Ehrenburg a quarter of a century earlier, and for rather similar reasons. He made friends easily among artists and writers everywhere, especially among the European Left.

His ebullience was unmistakeably genuine. He took us to shop for food in the covered Georgian market, where it was possible to buy fresh vegetables even in the depths of winter, a rarity in those days. He bought a huge slab of beef for our lunch, and a string of dried mushrooms for me, so strange in their beauty that I absolutely could not imagine putting them into soup as he suggested. Once back in Cambridge, I kept them so long in a tin they went mouldy before they could be used.

With the shopping complete, he took us back to his flat. He lived in one of the huge central blocks built of steel, stone and hard wood like the subway, which were once supposed to be set aside for Stakhanovite workers. There was none of the clutter we had seen in other Russian flats. In fact, it would have seemed bare if not for the art on his walls, notably a magnificent Blue Period Picasso. I stood in front of this for some time, before asking how he had come by it.

Smiling, he told the following story.

On a visit to Paris, in the early days of his own celebrity, he had been invited to meet Picasso in his studio. The painter was delighted with the lively, uninhibited young Russian and took him round his *atelier* before offering to give him any of the new paintings that he liked. Yevtushenko walked around, trying to decide, but found that none of the new paintings attracted him. To Picasso's amazement, he admitted this problem.

Picasso was not in the least offended. He chuckled: 'Until this moment I never really believed that Dostoevsky story about Nina Filipovna throwing a hundred thousand roubles into the fire – but now I see it is true. Simply Russian.'

We laughed, although I pointed out that the story in no way accounted for the Picasso on his wall.

'Ah. The following day I went round to meet Fernand Léger's widow, and told her the story. She beamed with glee. She felt Picasso had stolen much of the glory that belonged to Léger. 'You are right,' she said proudly. 'Everything Picasso does now is shit, *n'est ce pas?*'

Yevtushenko agreed politely, but then became aware of a picture on the wall of her flat, a painting of a woman at an ironing board. With as little tact as he had shown Picasso, he pointed to it and confessed: 'But *that* I do like.'

Her gaze followed his finger.

'*Like* it? You can *have* it,' she said, and there and then made to take it from the wall.

Yevtushenko helped her and accepted the gift happily, which was how the painting came to be hanging in his flat.

The following day he took us to meet his ex-wife, the flamboyant poet Bella Akhmadulina, who was living with her third husband, the stage designer Boris Messerer, in a huge flat which was attached to the Bolshoi Theatre. I remember a long corridor filled with props: many varieties of old flat irons, buckets, tongs, and metal fenders.

Yevtushenko ushered us through the flat into the huge kitchen and there, on the oak table, were little pewter saucepans filled with the same dish of chicken liver and nuts that we had eaten at the Writers' Union.

At the stove stood Akhmadulina, the Queen of Moscow poets. I thought she had gone to a great deal of trouble, and said so. Yevtushenko said glumly: 'She didn't cook for me.'

I believed him. She is a striking beauty and her poems do not suggest she could ever have made a conventional wife. In one poem she is a woman in a fever, burning and shaking so fiercely that the doctor can hardly examine her. Her neighbours are disgusted by her strangeness. In 'Rain', she arrives at a smart party soaked through, and is brought up to the fire by her disapproving hostess to dry out. The eager cries of the guests remind her of the way a crowd would once have urged a witch into the flames. Even more than Tsvetaeva, she relishes the thought of having supernatural powers.

Yevtushenko called her writing of 'I swear' an inner Rubicon. In this short fierce poem she gives the name of Yelabuga, the little town on the Kama where Marina Tsvetaeva took her own life, to a fairytale monster which she threatens to kill:

> Then the green juice of her young will burn
> the soles of my feet with their poison, but I'll
> hurl the egg that ripens in her tail
> into the earth, the bottomless earth…

The poem ends with the Yelabuga turning a single yellow eye in the poet's direction. These are poems which could easily be read politically, and Akhmadulina has often courted trouble, but there is something playful in her. And she is never altogether reverent. Hers is a genuine Tatar name – unlike Akhmatova's which was assumed when her father objected to her writing poetry – and Bella enjoyed making that clear. They had never been close friends. Akhmadulina told a story about one of her rare meetings with Akhmatova. She had offered to drive the ageing poet to a dacha close to Moscow but unfortunately Akhmadulina's car stalled at the traffic lights and, despite a desperate struggle with the starting handle, lifting the bonnet and calling on the help of several passers by, the journey ended ignominiously. Akhmadulina drew herself up to her full height, to mime Akhmatova's magnificence as she decisively refused the offer of a lift in a friend's car: 'I never make the same mistake twice.'

I had one further task to perform while I was in Moscow. Before leaving London, the playwright Michael Frayn, whom I know only casually, had asked me to find out what was happening to his Russian translator, Nyella, who was in some kind of difficulty. He had suggested I should not telephone from the hotel, so on our last day I asked Masha if I could use her mother's telephone.

Nyella answered nervously, and was alarmed when she heard I was from London. Immediately she plied me with a flurry of questions. I was unable to answer any of them. Frayn and I were far from close, and not only did I not know the name of Frayn's first wife, I had no idea how many children he had. I was afraid she would hang up on me.

Before she could do so, Masha took the telephone and explained that I was phoning from the flat of Margarita Aliger, and that I was a trusted friend. Nyella then gave me her address and I promised to go and see her on the evening before our flight home. My husband and I decided to go together.

Prospekt Vernadskovo. Somewhere in the northern suburbs. I did not at first recognise the address, though we had seen it before. In London. It was an address we had been given of a house where unofficial seminars took place for *refuseniks*, people who had applied for a visa to emigrate to Israel, and lost their jobs for doing so. Eminent scientists from abroad visited them, and distinguished writers too.

Since I knew that I would need several future visas to complete my Tsvetaeva biography, I had decided not to give the authorities such an easy opportunity of refusing me entry. I had even taken the typed address out of my luggage in case it was searched. Now I was travelling towards the very house, and quite soon very noisily.

Prospekt Vernadskovo was out in snowy suburbs, where no one cleared the snow as they did in central Moscow. There were frozen piles to the height of a house on each side of the road, though little channels had been dug at intervals through the thick walls so that people could make their way through to their homes. In the starlight, the snow had a blue gleam, and there was little traffic. The temperature had fallen far below zero.

Once in Prospekt Vernadskovo itself, there was an unexpected problem. We knew the house was Dom 99, but the numbering of Russian streets follows no obvious order. Several times our taxi paused and our driver ran through a channel to check the house numbers, only to come back shaking his head. Several times we had to turn in our tracks. We could hear him shouting to an occasional resident. It was getting late. My thoughts began to turn apprehensively to our early morning plane.

Then a large, bear-like figure of a man dressed in a furry coat flagged us down. It was Volodya, Nyella's partner. We got out into knee-high snow, paid the taxi and followed Volodya into a block of flats, or rather bedsitters, where, as we soon discovered, an interesting group of people were living, among them the nephew of the artist Naum Gabo. Once they heard there was a visitor from the West, all the residents piled into Nyella's tiny sitting room bearing vodka and tins of sardines and made us welcome. They sat on bare floorboards between sticks of chairs, some broken.

All were *refuseniks*. Their poverty was obvious, but they were far from gloomy. I asked one of them, a young pale-skinned boy with narrow lips and a heartbreaking smile, why exactly he wanted to go to Israel. He was astonished. 'Because being a Jew in Russia is not easy, of course,' he replied. 'To get into Moscow University, for instance, we need 10 per cent higher marks than an ethnic Russian. And the other students at the Conservatoire hate us. They learn it with their mother's milk. You won't understand that because you aren't Jewish.'

'But I *am*,' I replied. 'Surely I look more Jewish than you do, with my dark hair and black eyes?'

But he remained sceptical. I suppose each country recognises its outsiders by different clues.

'When, as a child, you hear the way they say *Yevrei*, something curls up within you for ever. It is worse than *Zhid*, which is almost friendly.'

He was not religious. He was a musician. There would be many such on the pavements of Tel Aviv once the floodgates opened.

We did not leave until it was time to go and collect our cases for the plane to London. As we left, Volodya gave us two black wooden carvings of a priest. A large one for Michael Frayn, and a smaller one for me. Much later, rumours of Volodya's activities as an icon smuggler reached me.

29 Odessa 2005

Odessa is Isaac Babel's town.

The stucco has gone from the painted houses of the Moldovanka, and the streets are very poor; washing is pinned up outside the balconies of cheap flats; the courtyards are mean, with a standpipe for water in each of them. Few people are walking around. No sign of Babel's rumbustious carters, or his gangster hero Benya Krik, wearing a chocolate jacket, cream pants and red boots. But people still point out the place where Benya Krik held a party so large that it spilled across the pavement.

Not that Babel grew up in the Moldovanka. There is a plaque outside his parents' house in Richelevskaya Boulevard, a merchant's house, in the centre of town, and he spent his childhood in the Black Sea village of Nikolaev. After the Civil War, he lived in Moscow, dreaming of poppy seed bread and sunshine. But his stories gave Odessa a new image of itself, rather as Damon Runyon or Woody Allen gave a flavour to Manhattan.

In Babel's day the port attracted ships from Newcastle, Marseilles and Port Said. On the docks these days there are gangsters far less benevolent than Benya Krik, who could get what he wanted with soft words rather than violence and sometimes shot his bullets into the air. The new hoods kidnap pretty young girls and ship them across to Turkey to work as prostitutes. The novelist Andrei Kurkov, who wrote *Death and the Penguin*, once planned to make a TV film about the practice but was warned off sharply. Even after the Orange Revolution, the Ukraine is still run by the Mafia.

'You don't bother them, they won't bother you,' I was told. Not all their activities are sinister. Odessa was once the centre of the illegal antiquities trade, and young men still hang around the archaeological museum offering impeccable forgeries of ancient Greek sculptures. There was even a time when wealthy gangsters supported pet writers or put money into Art Films. Such backing was not without risk. Kurkov told me of one director who took some of this Mafia money for his own use and was shot dead for his impudence.

In September 2005, I travelled to Odessa with my eldest son, Adam, and we stayed at the Londonskaya Hotel on Primorsky Boulevard, a cobbled esplanade at the top of the famous Odessa Steps. These lead down to Morsky Voksal, an ugly one-storey building from which ships leave for towns around the Black Sea. The main dock highway runs along the foot of the steps and the sea is nearly invisible behind the discoloured cement of the ocean terminals. People walk along Primorsky constantly. The centre of Odessa is built for strolling around and staring. From Primorsky it is only a few minutes to Deribasovskaya Street.

The Londonskaya Hotel itself was built in 1827 and has high ceilings, chandeliers and curving balustrades. Writers have always liked to stay there – Chekhov and Essenin among them – and the hotel proudly puts photographs outside the rooms they once occupied. It was popular with the NKVD in Soviet times, too; indeed, they commandeered the whole of the ground floor, and one of the poets we met – Boris Hersonsky – recalled two spells of interrogation there.

Odessa is a provincial city – the capital of the Ukraine is the ancient city of Kiev – but it has something of the grandeur of a southern St Petersburg. It was built at the command of Catherine the Great. Joseph de Ribas, an adventurer and womaniser, conquered the land; French and Italian architects built the city on what was said to be the site of a Greek town called Odessos, after Odysseus. In fact, the Greek colony is farther along the coast and the city was probably named for Catherine's current Greek lover. There are other stories, but only one undisputed fact: at a court ball in 1795, Catherine declared that, since the city had been founded by a woman, it should be given a feminine gender.

So Odessa was born. A free port of traders: Greeks, Turks and Tatars; Cossacks too, a band of deserters grown into a people with their own tradition of freedom and ferocity. Jews from the *stetls* at the western edge of the Russian Empire were invited in by the Duc de Richelieu, the governor of the city from 1803 to 1814, who thought they would make good merchants. They soon understood that Odessa was a city of immigrants, rather like New York. Their children were allowed into Russian schools.

It is easy to see why Zaida loved the town. The climate of Odessa is benign. Some winters there is no snow, and spring always comes early. In the late afternoon, the air is warm and scented with Mediterranean flowers. There are cafés on the pavements of Deribasovskaya Ulitsa, an opera house, a theatre. In the centre, street life is rich and in Babel's day *luftmenschen* wandered through the coffee houses, trying to con a rouble or two from the patrons by some trick or other. There were Jewish women selling live chickens, Greeks selling coffee and spice, German sausage-makers, Rumanians playing music in the streets.

By the time Zaida reached the city, nearly half the population were Jews. Most were poor, but they were loud, energetic, confident. A little later in the century, some owned newspapers; others wrote for them, like Vladimir Jabotinsky, the radical Zionist. By then there was a Bohemian, well-heeled Jewish middle class. Meetings of Zionists took place in a Viennese style building near the Opera House now called Hotel Mozart.

Adam and I, after our travels in northern Russia two years earlier, were bemused by the sunshine. On Primorsky Boulevard, the chestnut and plane trees were not yet autumnal. We met a man carrying two live rabbits in his arms and, as we stared, he advanced to sell them to us. Later, as we walked up towards the market, there were stranger creatures on offer: one resembling a baby crocodile, with a string securing its long mouth. Perhaps an unusual lizard? Perhaps the mythical salamander? A greeny-grey creature.

We sat in a café called Druzhya i Pivo ('Friends and beer') with chessboards marked on its tables. There we ate herring and sliced onion, with glasses of chilled Stella Artois. There was an illusory sense of Western prosperity. The girls walking by were unexpectedly well-dressed, which must have been a matter of pride rather than spare cash, since most jobs are very ill-paid.

We had not expected there to be many Jews left in the Ukraine after the massacres, so the number of writers, teachers and television pundits with a Jewish history was startling. They were not survivors exactly, but people returning to the city and remaining there even when it was possible to leave. Even after 1989, when so many left for Israel – Haifa is a short boat trip away – the census recorded 69,100 Jews remaining. Even now there are more than 40,000 in the city and in September 2005 there was a Jewish mayor. However, the majority of Jews are poor, old and dependent on soup kitchens for their food. These are largely run by synagogues, the most famous of which is the Brodsky Synagogue, a majestic building in Florentine Gothic at the corner of Pushkinskaya and Zhukovskaya Streets. It was named after Jews from the town of Brody in the Austro-Hungarian Empire, a Reform congregation. The cantor was said to have a splendid voice, and there was a choir and an organ – this last forbidden to an Orthodox community. Mussorgsky once came to listen to the music there, and it was the preferred synagogue of the Jewish intelligentsia until 1925, when the Soviet authorities closed it down along with other places of worship. Then it fell into disuse. The building has been restored with the help of American money from the Lubavitch Foundation: mahogany, thick carpets, chandeliers. Brass plaques announce individual donors. It is now ultra-Orthodox. Apart from the *shammes*, and a middle-aged woman who managed the gift shop, however, there was no one from the congregation when we put our noses inside.

Even in the middle of the afternoon, the synagogue on Yevraiskaya Street is livelier. Young boys laugh and smoke cigarettes on the steps. Inside, we found a young teacher with a parchment-yellow face, gingery hair and big, melancholy eyes. He had been born in Belorus, where Jews were commonly attacked physically. It was rather better, he told us, in Odessa. When he said something ironic, a grin transformed his whole face with amusement.

Every morning, old, poor Jews, mainly women, come to the synagogue for free food and to pray. When we returned on our last morning, I met an old man with a black beard and deep-set eyes whose face crinkled up when he smiled. His heavy build, his ready shrug and the way his cardigan rode up at the back reminded me of Zaida in spite of his different colouring.

He came from Zhitomir, a city in Western Ukraine, some time under Polish, some time in Lithuanian control, with a long history of pogrom and persecution. The brilliant Yiddish writer Mendele Mocher Sforim lived there, and Chaim Bialik grew up nearby. The young men from Zhitomir were less passive than those in other small towns in 1905. When anti-Jewish riots broke out, in the wake of the Beilis Trial, organised groups of Zionist and Socialist young men fought back, though several lost their lives doing so.

Babel described Zhitomir as it was when Poles had taken the town for a time. The Polish soldiers organised a pogrom, cut off beards, cut out tongues. The people were glad to see the Cossacks ride into town. Perhaps the Bolsheviks would prove saviours? He saw women washing clothes in the river, and old Jewish men with long skinny legs soaping themselves. The Civil War was raging. A shopkeeper in a Dickensian shop, recognising him as a Jew, muttered to him: 'They all say they are fighting for justice, and they all loot.'

Strangely, the man we met from Zhitomir remembered an idyllic childhood as the son of a cobbler, with everything a large family could need. In Soviet times he worked on the shop floor of a factory. In the Second World War he was at the Front. His parents had survived because they were evacuated to Uzbekistan. I guessed he must be at least eighty-five, though he still looked sturdy.

'Well,' he smiled, 'my only work nowadays is to come twice a day to the synagogue.'

He had a daughter in New York and I wondered why he was not tempted to join her.

'And how would the synagogue survive without me?' he demanded.

These ghosts of a lost world make jokes as if they are amused by God. Enduring so many vicissitudes, they feel entitled to question Him. Theirs is a religion of questions, always posed with irony.

This is a bitter amusement, but not a defensive one; no emotions are denied or hidden; it holds the full knowledge of human brutality and helplessness, alongside a profound gratitude for being alive.

It is Babel's irony.

30 Brodsky

I met Joseph Brodsky for the first time in London, on his way out of the Soviet Union, when he looked through my translations of Tsvetaeva, murmuring the lines of her poems which he had by heart. It was an unnerving experience, and it did not go well. He thought her the greatest of Russian poets, alongside Mandelstam, and he wanted her rhymes and metres preserved in English.

We saw more of one another when he came to take up a Fellowship at Clare Hall. He was lonely in Cambridge, which is not particularly hospitable to poets – even Octavio Paz, that most charming and gregarious of diplomats found as much – and it is to that loneliness I attribute Joseph's occasional visits, and the meals he took at my house. Sometimes he watched football with my youngest son, Joel, who was much the same age as the son he had been forced to leave in Russia.

When I met him again in New York in 1978, he was living in a flat in Greenwich Village. I had come to interview him for the *Sunday Times* as part of a piece that included Andrei Sinyavsky and the Chilean José Donoso, to be called 'Writers in Exile'.

Later, at the Cambridge Poetry Festival, we clashed on a television panel, in which he argued about the necessity for rhyme in translating Russian verse. I explained that in English verse there is a quite different tradition, in which the shape of every line has to pull against the rhythms of colloquial speech; and more is lost than gained by insisting on strong full rhymes. I said, 'You can't preserve all that.'

He retorted with a joke about the taxi driver, who, when asked how to get to Carnegie Hall, replies, 'Practise. Practise. Practise.'

My indignation was profound.

'Practise? You mean Shakespeare? Milton? Wordsworth? Eliot?'

The audience was restive. They wanted to hear Brodsky talk about Mandelstam.

He was rude, brusque, annoyed by my presumption and that evening did not show up at a supper party in his honour, perhaps most irritated by our conversation in the bar after the panel, when several poets, notably Vasco Popa, declared themselves on my side in defence of modernism. At the Festival, he read in a magnetic, mesmerising way, which those who read the translations did not attempt to mimic.

He bore me no ill will. I happened to be in New York on the very day he first heard that he would need a bypass. He drove me to the airport and shared his thoughts about the possibility of death.

'Afterwards there is only the book,' he said.

31 Heaven

No golden floors, no feathery
    seraphim. Only a garden
where two people are reading
    under a eucalyptus tree.

It is London, pale sunshine,
    here and now. Already
we are their immortality.
    Their spirits enter us,

and those who come after,
    in other cities, other languages.
May the Lord in his long silence
    remember all of us.

Notes

Italic in the text indicates direct quotation from Russian writers.

Akhmadulina, Bella (1937–)

Izabella Akhatovna Akhmadulina is a Russian-language poet of Tatar and Italian descent. She is one of the most distinctive voices of her generation, a great beauty, and the first wife of Yevgeny Yevtushenko. She is a member of the Writers' Union, even though she was willing to publish alongside writers in trouble with the Party and always declared her reverence for the work of poets such as Anna Akhmatova and Marina Tsvetaeva, who attracted official disapproval. She now lives with her third husband, Boris Messerer, a theatre designer, in Moscow.

Akhmatova, Anna (1889–1966), née Gorenko

Akhmatova is an iconic figure in twentieth-century Russian literature. Her lyrics of unhappy love were known across Russia before the First World War. Many men fell in love with her beauty, and even in old age she was surrounded by young men who loved her genius. She was one of the first to understand the brutality of the Soviet regime, when her first husband, Nikolai Gumilyov, was executed by the Bolsheviks in 1921. During the years of Stalin's Terror, she was forbidden to publish, and her only son and her third husband were held in the Gulag to ensure her silence. At a time when every scrap of paper could be used as evidence, she and her friends learned the lyrics of 'Requiem' by heart before burning them in an ashtray. She was fortunate to outlive Stalin, and in the last years of her life received several honours, including an honorary doctorate from Oxford University.

Akiba, Rabbi Ben Joseph

A learned Hebrew scholar and teacher of the late first and early second century AD. He showed exemplary faith and courage even as he was flayed alive.

Aliger, Margarita Iosifovna (1915–1992)

A distinguished poet and journalist, born in Odessa. After completing a chemistry degree, she studied at the Gorky Institute for Literature from 1934 to 1937 and became a famous Soviet poet, essayist and journalist. She wrote about the heroism of the Soviet people during the Second World War. Her most celebrated poem, 'Zoya', is about a young Russian girl killed by the Nazis. There are other more personal themes, however, including the French exile of Marina Tsvetaeva, and her own loneliness.

Aragon, Louis (1897–1982)

Aragon was a distinguished French poet, involved in the Dada and Surrealist movements, who joined the French Communist Party. In 1939, he married the Russian writer Elsa Triolet, and the couple worked for the French Underground under the German occupation.

Babel, Isaac (1894–1941)

Babel grew up in Nikolaev, close to Odessa. His father paid for violin lessons, hoping his son would prove a prodigy, but Isaac preferred to read French literature and wrote precocious stories in imitation of Guy de Maupassant. Refused entry to Odessa University – because there was a Jewish quota – he graduated from Kiev University in 1915 and then moved to St Petersburg. His first patron was Maxim Gorky, who published Babel's stories in his magazine *Letopis*. He went on to work for the Ukrainian State Publishing House. In the Civil War, he supported the Bolsheviks and rode alongside Field Marshall Budyonny's First Cavalry, well aware of the irony of a Jew riding alongside

Cossacks, who had been their historic enemy. The stories in *Red Cavalry* record the violence and courage he witnessed, the casual murder of Jews in their small villages, and his own inability to bring death to a wounded comrade. His clipped prose has an idiosyncratic purity. His fame rests on *Red Cavalry* and his *Tales of Odessa*, set in the Moldavanka, a colourful district of Odessa filled with many Jews and a few gangsters. He fell silent in the thirties, and in 1939 he was arrested and taken into prison. He was executed in 1941.

Benya Krik
In Isaac Babel's stories of Odessa, Benya Krik is the Jewish gangster who commands the greatest respect.

Berggoltz, Olga Fyodrovna (1910–1975)
An impressive Soviet poet, though remembered now mainly for her radio broadcasts throughout the siege of Leningrad in the Second World War.

Beria, Lavrenti (1899–1953)
Beria was born into a peasant family in the Abkhazian region of Georgia. He was the Chief of Soviet Police who presided over the last stages of Joseph Stalin's Great Purge of the 1930s. He was most influential during and after the Second World War. After Stalin's death, he was for a short time First Deputy Prime Minister. He was executed on the orders of Khrushchev in 1953.

Brodsky, Joseph (1940–1996)
Brodsky was the only child of a Leningrad Jewish family. His father was a photographer, his mother a teacher. He walked out of school at fifteen, and dedicated himself thereafter to writing poetry whilst doing menial jobs. He was recognised early by Akhmatova as a Russian poet of genius. When he was arrested and charged as a 'social parasite', his trial aroused international interest. He was condemned to internal exile in Arkangelskoye

in the far north and remained there from 1964 to 1965. In 1972, he was forced to go into exile in Austria. W.H. Auden befriended him there and he was later given a term's Fellowship at Clare Hall in Cambridge, England, before taking up a teaching post at Ann Arbor, Michigan. His English, though idiosyncratic, was excellent, and he wrote essays for the *New York Review of Books*, which also published his poems. America honoured him in many ways: he was given the prestigious MacArthur Award, an Honorary Doctorate at Yale, and elected to the post of American Poet Laureate. He was awarded the Nobel Prize for Literature in 1987. He married a young wife, Maria Sozzani, in 1990. They had a daughter, Anna Maria Anastasia. Brodsky died in 1996 and is buried in Venice.

Bukharin, Nikolai Ivanovich (1888–1938)
Bukharin was involved in revolutionary politics from 1905 onwards. He was taken into prison several times and went into exile, only returning to Russia during the February Revolution. He was a dedicated Bolshevik and after 1925 a loyal supporter of Joseph Stalin. For a time he was Chairman of the Comintern. In 1929, he was deprived of that post but took up the editorship of the key newspaper *Izvestia* ('News'). From this position he was able to help many writers including those, like Osip Mandelstam, in trouble with the authorities. He remained a supporter of Stalin, but that did not prevent his arrest, torture and trial for treason. He was executed in March 1938.

Bulgakov, Mikhail Afanasyevich (1891–1940)
Bulgakov was born in Kiev, Ukraine and enlisted in the White Army during the Civil War. Out of these experiences, he wrote his great play *Days of the Turbins*, which was, rather surprisingly, much loved by Joseph Stalin. None of his other plays were performed in his lifetime, however, and his novels went unpublished. His desperate letter to Stalin, asking to be allowed to emigrate if he was not allowed to publish, brought an

unexpected phone call from Stalin with the promise of some work in the theatre. His most famous novel is *The Master and Margarita*, in which a devil accompanied by a talking cat fascinates the citizens of Moscow. The eponymous Master is in prison, writing a novel about Jesus Christ; Margarita was inspired by Bulgakov's third wife, Yelena. He died of kidney failure in 1940.

Cheka
The Russian Secret Police after the Bolshevik Revolution, a precursor of the NKVD and KGB.

Clair, René (1898–1981)
Distinguished French film maker and scriptwriter, most celebrated for *Sous les Toits de Paris* and *À Nous la Liberté*.

Der Nister (1884–1950), pseudonym of Pinchas Kahanovitch
Der Nister (The Hidden, or 'Secret', One) was born in the Ukraine, and wrote novels and short stories influenced by Jewish mystical tradition. He left Russia to live in Germany in 1921, returning in 1927. His writing was condemned by the Soviet regime and he turned to journalism. During the Second World War he wrote about the destruction of Jewish life in Europe. He was arrested in 1949 and died in the Gulag.

Detskoye Selo
The Bolshevik name for Tsarskoye Selo, a suburb on the outskirts of Leningrad.

Dzerzhinsky, Feliks (1877–1926)
The son of a Polish nobleman, Dzerzhinsky became a fanatical Bolshevik, and was appointed first Head of the Soviet Secret Police.

Efron, Sergei (1895–1941)
Efron was the husband of the great poet Marina Tsvetaeva. He

was the child of idealistic revolutionaries; his mother an aristocrat, his father Jewish. Efron and Tsvetaeva married in 1912. They had two daughters and one son. Efron fought with the White Army in the Civil War, and went abroad when the war ended in Bolshevik victory. When Ehrenburg brought Tsvetaeva the news that her husband was still alive, Tsvetaeva at once decided to follow him to Prague where he was studying. Efron suffered from tuberculosis and when the family moved to Paris he was unable to find employment. He joined the Eurasian movement and helped to edit a magazine with strong ties to Soviet poets. This became a front for the NKVD. When the French police suspected he was involved in the murder of a Soviet defector, he was hastily taken back to Russia by Soviet agents. There he was given a house in Bolshevo, a suburb of Moscow. Shortly after Marina and her son Georgy returned to Russia, Efron and their daughter Alya were arrested. Alya was sentenced to hard labour, Efron imprisoned and then shot in 1941.

Efron, Alya (Ariadne Sergeevna) (1913–1975)
The eldest child of Marina Tsvetaeva, Alya was very gifted. She kept a brilliantly observant diary at the age of six. She also had considerable artistic talent. Tsvetaeva and Alya were always close, and their intimacy grew even more intense during the Civil War. In Prague, Alya was responsible for most domestic chores so that Tsvetaeva had time to write. In Paris, Alya moved closer to her father. She became a dedicated Communist in the thirties and, when she was given a visa, returned to Russia in 1937. Her father joined her later the same year when the NKVD brought him back to Russia. Alya was arrested and tortured in 1939 and, a month later, her father was arrested on her testimony. She was sentenced to the Gulag and not released until 1947. When it was possible, she worked to restore her mother's legacy. She died in July 1975.

Efron, Georgy Sergeevich (1925–1944)
Marina Tsvetaeva's youngest child, whom she adored and spoiled. He was handsome, intelligent, bilingual in French and Russian and eager to return to his homeland. He was often angry with his mother, and blamed the family's misfortunes on her. After Tsvetaeva's suicide, he was evacuated to Tashkent and there recorded in his diary the misery of his mother's last days. Called up in 1944, he was killed in his first battle.

Ehrenburg, Ilya (1891–1967)
Ehrenburg was a minor poet, a successful novelist and a journalist of genius. He was born in Kiev into a Jewish family. As a student in Moscow, he involved himself in anti-Tsarist agitation, spent a brief period in prison and then left Russia to live in exile in Paris. There he made friends with all the notable figures of the French *avant garde*. He lived as a freelance journalist, his small income supplemented by advances for his novels. His most popular novel was *The Extraordinary Adventures of Julio Jurenito and his Disciples* (1921) which in several ways prefigures Bulgakov's brilliant *The Master and Margarita*. In 1934, from the podium of the First Soviet Writers' Congress, he spoke in favour of Isaac Babel. He wrote regularly for *Izvestia*, notably from the front line in the Spanish Civil War. Though not a Bolshevik, he was vehemently opposed to Fascism. When Paris fell to the Germans in the Second World War, he escaped to Russia, at that time a German ally. When Germany invaded Russia, he worked as a war correspondent. His *Memoirs*, written in 'The Thaw' after Stalin's death, are probably his best work. He died of cancer in Moscow in 1967.

Eisenstein, Sergei Mikhailovich (1898–1948)
Film-maker and theorist, scriptwriter and editor, whose best known films are *Battleship Potemkin* and *October*.

Eurasianist Movement
The movement was founded in the 1920s by a handful of Russian

émigrés, including D.S. Mirsky, the literary critic. Their magazine published writers from Soviet Russia – such as Babel and Pasternak – as well as those like Tsvetaeva, living in exile. The NKVD saw its usefulness, and began to offer funds.

Fadeev, Alexander Alexandrovich (1901–1956)

A successful novelist and an underground fighter. In 1926, he was appointed to the executive of the Association of Proletarian Writers. His most popular novel, *The Rout* (1927), follows the fate of a group of revolutionary soldiers in flight from Cossacks at the time of the Japanese intervention in the Civil War. As Secretary of the Writers' Union all through Stalin's great purges, he signed the death warrants of many of Russia's best writers, including Osip Mandelstam. An alcoholic, he became seriously depressed towards the end of his life and killed himself in 1956, the year Khrushchev made his speech confessing the extent of Stalin's crimes. In his suicide note, he wrote of his despair when he remembered those who had been slaughtered.

Gorbachev, Mikhail Sergeevich (1931–)

Gorbachev was the General Secretary of the Soviet Communist Party from 1985 to 1991. He was responsible for initiating reforms of Communism which were much praised in the West but disliked by many in the Soviet Union. In 1991, a group of hard-line Communists attempted a coup; however, the citizens of Moscow linked arms in his support against their troops, and Boris Yeltsin bravely mounted a tank to appeal to the soldiers. When the coup failed, Gorbachev was succeeded by Yeltsin.

Gorky, Maxim (1868–1936), pseudonym of Alexei Maximovich Peshkov

Gorky chose his pseudonym, which means 'bitter', to reflect his anger at the harsh conditions of Russian life under the Tsar. An orphan from the age of ten, brought up by his grandmother, his first book of stories brought him success and he went on to become a world-famous writer. He was a personal friend of Lenin, but his newspaper *Novaya Zhisn* ('New Life') was censored by the Bolsheviks and he was unable to prevent the execution of the poet Nikolai Gumilyov in 1921. Soon afterwards, he went to live in Italy. His return to Russia in 1929 was a major coup for the Soviet regime. A central street in Moscow was given his name and much of the horror of the purges of the 1930s was concealed from him. Indeed, special editions of *Pravda* were printed for him daily so that he would not read about the trials and deaths of his friends. In 1935, Gorky's son died in suspicious circumstances and in 1936 Gorky also died. Poisoning has always been rumoured.

Goslitizdat
A publishing house.

Gumilyov, Nikolai Stepanovich (1886–1921)
A fine poet and a courageous explorer of Africa. He was in love for many years with Anna Akhmatova and married her in 1910. They had one son, Lev. Soon after their honeymoon he became openly unfaithful. Together with Osip Mandelstam and Akhmatova, he was part of a new movement of poetry which they called 'Acmeism', which stressed the importance of precision and rejected the mists of Symbolism. Akhmatova left her husband to live with the noted Babylonian scholar Vladimir Shileiko and she and Gumilyov divorced. Never a supporter of the Bolshevik Revolution, Gumilyov was not involved in any plot against it. Nevertheless, he was arrested in August 1921 and executed in the same year. He was the first poet to die at the hands of the Revolution.

Inber, Vera Mikhailovna (1890–1972)
A writer who lived for a time in Paris and Switzerland but returned to Moscow, she is best known for her remarkable diary of life during the Great Siege of Leningrad, where she remained throughout almost three years.

Jabotinsky, Vladimir (1880–1940)
Jabotinsky was born into an Odessa Jewish family. He became a fervent Zionist after the 1903 massacre of Jews in Kishinyov. A brilliant linguist, writer and orator, he wrote poems and novels even as he worked to convince the Diaspora to leave for Palestine. He was also the inspiration for Irgun, the terrorist arm of the Jewish Resistance movement in the 1940s.

Kerensky, Alexander Fyodorovich (1881–1970)
A dominant figure in the Russian provisional government set up by the February Revolution of 1917. This was overthrown by Lenin in the October Revolution of the same year.

Kholkozniks
Agricultural workers on collective farms.

Khrushchev, Nikita Sergeevich (1894–1971)
Khrushchev became the First Secretary of the Communist Party after the power struggle following Stalin's death. Seemingly a loyal supporter of Stalin while the dictator lived, it was Khrushchev who shocked the delegates to the Twentieth Party Congress in 1956 with an account of Stalin's crimes. When ousted from power in 1964, he was allowed to live quietly until his death, albeit under KGB surveillance.

Lenin (originally Ulyanov), Vladimir Ilyich (1870–1924)
Born into an educated family in Simbirsk on the Volga, he excelled at school, though he was expelled from university for his radical views, and his brother was executed for them. He spent many years in exile in Western Europe, but returned in 1917 and was the mastermind behind the October Revolution. In 1918, he survived an assassination attempt. In power, Lenin was ruthless but pragmatic, and introduced a measure of private enterprise to supplement the failing Marxist economy. He was uncertain about the wisdom of allowing Stalin to gain power. He died in 1924.

Lubianka

The popular name for the headquarters of the KGB prison on Lubianka Square in Moscow. This was built in 1898 for an insurance company but in Soviet times was a prison where gruesome tortures were practised daily.

Luftmenschen

A Yiddish word, literally meaning 'men of air' used to describe men who live on their wits.

Mandelstam, Osip Emilyevich (1891–1938)

A Russian poet generally regarded as one of the greatest voices of the twentieth century. He was born in Warsaw into the family of a wealthy Jewish leather merchant and grew up in St Petersburg, where he attended the prestigious Tenishev School. For a time he studied at St Petersburg University, though he did not graduate. He won fame in 1913 with the publication of *Kamen* ('Stone') and, alongside his close friends Anna Akhmatova and Nikolai Gumilyov, was one of the founding members of the Acmeist movement. He approved of the February Revolution in 1917 which established the Provisional Government, but was alarmed when the Bolsheviks seized power. He spent much of the subsequent Civil War in Southern Russia. In 1922, he married Nadezhda Iakolevna Khazin. As the Soviet authorities became suspicious of his loyalties, he began to find it hard to publish poetry and turned to prose. No poems were published between 1925 and 1930. His *Journey to Armenia* is the last major work published in his lifetime. He was arrested for the first time in 1934, after writing an epigram about Stalin. It was at this time that Stalin made a telephone call to Boris Pasternak to ask for his assessment of Mandelstam's genius. Pasternak hesitated. Mandelstam was exiled to Cherdyn in the Urals, where he attempted suicide. His sentence was commuted to exile in Voronezh, but in May 1938 he was arrested again and charged with counter-revolutionary activities. This time he was sentenced to five years. He died in a camp near Vladivostock on 27 December 1938. In 1970, his wife Nadezhda published memoirs of their life together which found an international audience.

Mariinski Theatre
A theatre in St Petersburg which is one of the best opera houses in the world and the home of the Kirov Ballet Company.

Meyerhold, Vsevolod (1874–1940)
Both his parents were Prussian citizens. At the age of twenty-one, Meyerhold converted from Lutheranism to the Russian Orthodox Church. A great theatrical innovator, he worked for the Moscow Arts Theatre, and made a decisive break with realism.

Mikhoels, Solomon (Schloime) (1890–1948)
A Jewish actor who played roles as diverse as Tevye the Milkman and King Lear. In 1920, he set up the Moscow State Jewish Theatre, which performed many Yiddish classics. During the Second World War, as a member of the Jewish Anti-Fascist Committee, he travelled to the United States to raise money for the Soviet cause. His horror at Nazi atrocities made him keen to see Ehrenburg's *Black Book of Soviet Jewry* published in Russia, and he was sympathetic to the State of Israel. He died in a car accident arranged by the KGB in 1948.

Moldovanka
A poor district of Odessa, once filled with colourful gangsters.

Moritz, Yunna (1937–)
Yunna Moritz was born in Kiev. Her father, Pinchas Moritz, was imprisoned under Stalin. She spent the Second World War in the Urals, and became prominent as a poet as part of the sixties generation alongside Yevtushenko. Aside from the popularity of

her own poems, she is the translator of Constantine Cavafy and Federico García Lorca. She lives in Moscow.

Mussorgsky, Modest Petrovich (1839–1881)
A celebrated Russian composer who included a musical impression of a conversation between two Jews in his *Pictures from an Exhibition.*

Naiman, Anatoly Genrikhovich (1936–)
A poet, novelist, critic and translator, Anatoly Naiman has held Fellowships at both Harvard and Oxford, and has written significant memoirs of Anna Akhmatova. E.F. interviewed him when she was writing her own biography of Akhmatova. He lives in Moscow.

Nomenklatura
An élite of Communist Party members, often bureaucrats, who enjoyed special privileges.

Pasternak, Boris (1890–1960)
Boris Pasternak was born in Moscow into the Jewish family of a distinguished painter, Leonid Pasternak, and a gifted pianist, Rosa Kauffman. At first, he was attracted to a career as a composer but decided instead to go to the University of Marburg to study Philosophy. During the First World War, fired by a love affair, he wrote a sequence of poems, *My Sister Life,* which inspired a whole generation of poets, including Osip Mandelstam and Marina Tsvetaeva. At first, he was optimistic about the idealism of the Bolshevik Revolution, though not the Soviet insistence on Socialist Realism. He began a fervent correspondence with the great poet Marina Tsvetaeva, then in exile, after reading her sequence of lyrics from *Poem of the End.* Through his father, he was able to bring the German poet Rainer Maria Rilke into their correspondence. By the late 1920s, he found it hard to publish his own poetry in Russia and turned to prose, notably *Safe Conduct.*

157

A visit to the Ukraine, during which he witnessed the horrors of forced collectivisation, brought on a nervous breakdown. During the great purges of the 1930s, he began to work on the translation of Shakespeare's plays, which became immensely popular. Even Stalin admired his poetry, and was said to have crossed his name off a list of those to be arrested, saying: 'Leave this cloud dweller alone.' It was under Khrushchev in 1958 that Pasternak allowed his novel *Dr Zhivago* to be published in Italy by the Feltrinelli publishing house. It brought him worldwide fame. A year later, he was named as the winner of the Nobel Prize for Literature. As his poetry was cited rather than his novel, he at first accepted joyfully, and then was brought to refuse. The Party, incensed at his disloyalty, demanded he should be sent into exile, but the sentence was revoked. He died of cancer in 1960.

Pasternak, Leonid Osipovich (1862–1945)
Leonid Pasternak was born into a Jewish family in Odessa and became a celebrated Russian painter, particularly noted for his portraits: Lev Tolstoy and Rainer Maria Rilke both sat for him. His wife, Rosalie Kauffman, was a musical prodigy. He was the father of three daughters, who left Russia with him for Berlin in 1921, and two sons, who remained in Russia. One of his sons was the great poet Boris Pasternak.

Peredelkino
A village a few miles outside Moscow where the Writers' Union allocated dachas of different sizes to significant writers.

Pilnyak, Boris (pseudonym of Boris Andreyevich Vogau) (1894–1937)
His *Tale of the Unextinguished Moon* (1926) aroused criticism when it appeared; the magazine which included it was immediately banned. Since he drew a sympathetic portrait of a supporter of Leon Trotsky in his novel *Mahogany*, and allowed the book to be published abroad, the book was refused publication in the Soviet

158

Union. He continued to write, however, until in 1937 he disappeared. It is assumed he was arrested by the NKVD and executed.

Rachmones
A Hebrew word meaning compassion, which entered Yiddish speech.

Rashi, Rabbi Shlomo Yitzchak (1040–1105)
An outstanding scholar, translator and biblical commentator who lived in France in the Middle Ages.

Raskolnikov
The central figure in Dostoevsky's *Crime and Punishment*. He is a poor student who murders an old pawnbroker and is led by the cleverness of Inspector Porfiry to betray his own guilt.

Rein, Yevgeny Borisovich (1935–)
A distinguished Russian poet, winner of the prestigious Pushkin Prize, he was a friend of Akhmatova and also of Brodsky. They were both dubbed 'Akhmatova's Orphans' when she died.

Reiss, Ignace (1899–1937)
An important Soviet spy, who defected to the West and was assassinated in Lausanne on the orders of Yezhov in 1937.

Rilke, Rainer Maria (1875–1926)
One of the greatest poets in the German language, Rilke was born in Prague. In 1895, he made a trip to Russia, where he met Tolstoy and the Russian painter Leonid Pasternak (the father of the poet Boris Pasternak). It was through his father that Boris Pasternak made epistolary contact with a poet he revered. Marina Tsvetaeva, with whom Boris was also in correspondence, eagerly joined in an exchange of letters with Rilke during the last months of his life.

Rushniki
Long, embroidered towels.

Ryleev, Kondraty Fedorovich (1795–1826)
A leadingDecembrist poet, Ryleev was executed at the command of Nicholas I. He was a friend of Alexander Pushkin.

Shammes
A 'man of all work' connected to a synagogue, with a role somewhere between that of a beadle and a caretaker.

Stalin (originally Dzhugashvili), Joseph Vissarionovich (1879–1953)
Born into a cobbler's family in Gory, Georgia, Stalin was educated at a theological seminary. He was an early worker for the Revolution, though he did not have a central position in 1917. He was appointed General Secretary of the Party in 1922, and by the end of the 1920s had outmanoeuvred all his rivals. His enforced collectivisation of agriculture cost millions of lives, and in the 1930s he organised the Great Terror, supposedly designed to rid the Party of its enemies. He concluded a pact with Hitler in 1939 and was ill-prepared for Hitler's invasion. Nevertheless, his ruthless indifference to human losses led his country to victory and after the Second World War his empire extended over most of Eastern Europe. In the last years of his life, he became increasingly paranoid. He died in 1953.

Sviatopolk-Mirsky, Dmitry Petrovich (1890–1939)
A political and literary historian, who emigrated to Great Britain in 1921, renouncing his title of Prince. While teaching Russian Literature at the University of London, he wrote a *History of Russian Literature from its Beginnings* which remains a standard textbook. He returned to the Soviet Union in the thirties as a convinced Marxist. He was arrested in Moscow in 1937 and died in a camp in the Gulag in 1939.

Taganka
A Moscow theatre with a small auditorium where in Soviet times the seats were reserved for Union members or Western visitors.

Talisim
Prayer shawls.

Tenishev School
A school in St Petersburg famous for its Western, liberal ideals. Many important writers, such as Vladimir Nabokov, attended.

Tsvetaeva, Marina Ivanovna (1892–1941)
One of the greatest Russian poets of the twentieth century, and arguably the most original. Born in Moscow into the family of Ivan Tsvetsaev, Professor of Fine Arts at Moscow University, she grew up in material comfort. Her childhood, however, was dominated by the ferocious puritanism of her mother Maria, who had married a much older widower only because her father refused to let her marry the man she loved. Denied a career as a concert pianist herself, Maria forced her elder daughter to spend hours at the piano every day from the age of six. Maria had tuberculosis and died when Marina was fourteen; her daughter then abandoned the study of the piano and began to write poetry. She said: 'After a mother like that, I had only one alternative: to become a poet.' By the age of eighteen, Tsvetaeva already had a reputation as a poet and could number the poet Maximilian Voloshin among her friends. It was at Voloshin's dacha in the Crimea that she met Sergei Efron. They married in 1912 and before war broke out in 1914 they had two children, and were inordinately happy. Tsvetaeva was not faithful to Efron, however: she had a brief love affair with Osip Mandelstam and a longer and more intense relationship with the lesbian poet Sofia Parnok. In the Civil War, Efron went south to fight for the White Army; Tsvetaeva remained in Moscow coping with two young children through the Moscow famine. She was particularly close

to her precocious elder daughter Ariadne (Alya). When the situation was at its most desperate, Tsvetaeva put her younger daughter Irina into an orphanage, where the child died of malnutrition in 1919. After the Civil War ended in victory for the Bolsheviks in 1922, Efron fled to Prague. When Ehrenburg brought Tsvetaeva the news her husband was still alive, she immediately made the decision to join him. There followed a long period of exile, in Prague and in Paris, where she saw her early fame vanish. Her most intense erotic experience was a brief love affair with Konstantin Rodzevich in Prague and she records the end of their love in 'Poem of the Mountain' and 'Poem of the End'. Afterwards, with her husband, she had a son, Georgy, nicknamed Moor, on whom she lavished all her affection. In Paris, her daughter Alya became much closer to her father and, as a convinced Communist, chose to return to Russia. When Efron was exposed as a Soviet agent in 1937, the NKVD hastily took him back to Russia. Tsvetaeva knew nothing of his activities as a spy but she was ostracised by the Russian émigré community in Paris nevertheless. Tsvetaeva followed Efron back to Russia with Moor in 1939. Alya was arrested only months after Tsvetaeva's return and Efron – incriminated by Alya under torture – a month later. Desolate, Tsvetaeva went to Moscow to look for old friends but most were afraid to meet her. When the Germans invaded Russia, Tsvetaeva took Georgy and herself to Yelabuga on the River Kama, close to Chistopol where the Writers' Union evacuated its members. In her loneliness, and after a quarrel with Moor, Tsvetaeva hanged herself in 1941.

Yagoda, Genrikh Grigorievich (1891–1938)

Yagoda was born in Rybinsk into a Jewish family and joined the Bolsheviks in 1907. He rose through the ranks of the Cheka to become Deputy to Feliks Dzershinsky and in 1934 Joseph Stalin appointed Yagoda People's Commissar for Internal Affairs. Yagoda oversaw the interrogation process leading to the first Moscow Show Trial and the subsequent execution of former

Soviet leaders Grigory Zinoviev and Lev Kamenev in August 1936. However, on 16 September 1936, Yagoda was replaced by Nikolai Yezhov and in March 1937 was arrested and found guilty of treason. After another show trial in March 1938, he was executed by shooting.

Yaponchik, Misha
A famous Odessa gangster, who was one of the models for Isaac Babel's character Benya Krik.

Yeltsin, Boris Nikolaevich (1931–2007)
Yeltsin was declared the first President of the Russian Federation in 1991 after his courage helped to defeat the coup against Gorbachev. By the time he left office, however, Yeltsin was deeply unpopular. His reforms devastated the living standards of much of the population, especially the groups dependent on Soviet-era State subsidies. Hyper-inflation wiped out personal savings. In 2000, he announced his resignation, leaving the presidency in the hands of Vladimir Putin. Yeltsin died in 2007.

Yevtushenko, Yevgeny Alexandrovich (1933–)
Yevtushenko is the best-known poet of the generation which grew up after Stalin's death. He was born in Irkutsk, Siberia. He came to Moscow to study at the Gorky Institute and published poetry which rapidly became hugely popular. He gave readings to audiences whose numbers could fill football stadiums and became a figure on the international stage with his poem 'Babiy Yar' (1961) which denounced both Nazi and Russian anti-Semitism. He was often outspoken, but both Khrushchev and Brezhnev saw he was a useful ambassador for Socialism and he was allowed to travel abroad widely. He sometimes took risks for his friends: the Nobel Prize winner Alexander Solzhenitsyn took shelter for a time at his flat. When the Soviet regime collapsed, and sales of all books diminished, he supplemented his income by teaching at the American University of Oklahoma.

Yezhov, Nikolai Ivanovich (1895–1940)
Yezhov replaced Yagoda as Head of the Secret Police from 1936 to 1938 during Stalin's greatest purges. He was only five foot tall, had a club foot and a reputation for taking pleasure in cruelty.

Zhdanov, Andrei Alexandrovich (1896–1948)
Andrei Zhdanov was born in Mariupol, Ukraine. He joined the Bolsheviks in 1915 and became a close associate of Joseph Stalin. After the assassination of Sergei Kirov in 1934, Stalin appointed Zhdanov as Governor of Leningrad. In this post he played an important role in the great purges that took place in the Communist Party between 1934 and 1941. After the war, he led the purge of non-conformist artists and intellectuals. Following his carefully worded decree in 1946, the Executive Committee expelled Anna Akhmatova and Mikhail Zoshchenko from the Union of Soviet Writers. He died in 1948.

Timeline

1903	Pogrom in Kishinyov.
1905	A peaceful demonstration of poor men and women, some with children, and led by the Russian Orthodox priest Father Gapon, presents a petition at the Winter Palace. They are fired on, and many killed. This sparks revolts across Russia, which are put down with great cruelty.
1914	First World War breaks out. In an initial wave of patriotism, St Petersburg is re-named Petrograd, to sound less Germanic.
1915–16	Great Russian losses at the Front, and many soldiers desert.
1917	After demonstrations, strikes and food riots, the February Revolution ousts Tsar Nicholas II and a Provisional Government is installed. Vladimir Ilyich Lenin returns to Russia travelling through Germany in a closed train.

The October Revolution by Bolsheviks, masterminded by Lenin, overthrows the Provisional Government. Russia makes a separate peace with Germany. |
1918	Civil War breaks out between Bolshevik and White armies. There is famine in Moscow and Petrograd and atrocities are committed by both sides in the Ukraine, Belorussia and Poland. Tsar Nicholas and his family are murdered in Yekaterinburg. Lenin survives an attempted assassination.
1921	Nikolai Gumilyov is accused of conspiracy and executed by Bolsheviks.
1922	The Civil War ends in Bolshevik victory. The White

Army disperses. Tsvetaeva travels to Prague to join her husband Efron.

1924   Death of Lenin. Joseph Stalin uses his position as General Secretary of the party to take over the leadership. Petrograd becomes Leningrad.

1928   Leon Trotsky, a Jewish intellectual and Stalin's rival, is banished to Kazakhstan, then departed from the Soviet Union.

1929   Nikolai Bukharin is made Editor of *Izvestia* ('News'). Stalin consolidates his position.

1934   The murder of Sergei Kirov, supposedly Stalin's good friend, becomes the occasion for the beginning of Stalin's Great Terror. Mandelstam is arrested. Stalin telephones Pasternak to ask whether Mandelstam is a poet of genius. Yagoda is appointed People's Commissar for Internal Affairs. Akhmatova's son Lev is arrested.

1936   Stalin's former colleagues Zinoviev and Kamenev are interrogated, publicly tried and executed. Yagoda is replaced by Yezhov. A civil War breaks out in Spain, after an attempt by General Franco and the army to overthrow the Republican Government. Nazi Germany and Fascist Italy support Franco. Maxim Gorky dies.

1937   Yagoda is arrested. In France, Sergei Efron is exposed as a Soviet agent and flees to Russia.

1938   Yagoda is tried and executed. Lavrenti Beria takes over his post. Mandelstam is arrested for the second time in May. He dies in a prison camp near Vladivostock in December.

1939   Tsvetaeva, ostracised by her fellow émigrés in Paris, returns with her son to Russia to join her husband and her daughter Alya. The Nazi Soviet pact, which dismays many Communist supporters in the rest of Europe, is agreed in August. In September, Hitler invades Poland, Russia occupies Eastern Poland, and the Second World War breaks out.

Germans invade and conquer France. Ilya Ehrenburg returns to Russia from Paris. The London Blitz begins.

1941   Germany invades Russia with great brutality, and lays siege to Leningrad. Akhmatova is evacuated from Leningrad; first to Chistopol, then to Tashkent. Isolated from her fellow writers, Tsvetaeva hangs herself in Yelabuga. In September, the Germans take Kiev, and begin to shoot civilians – mainly Jews but also Ukrainians, Gypsies and Prisoners of War. Their bodies are thrown into the ravine of Babiy Yar.

1942–3 Soviet armies fight the invaders with great courage and huge losses. The tide of the war begins to turn in favour of the Russians.

1945   At a meeting in Yalta in the Crimea, Churchill, Roosevelt and Stalin determine the shape of Europe after the war. Victory over Germany leaves the whole of Eastern Europe, including Poland, in Russian hands.

1946   Zhdanov's decree forces Akhmatova out of the Writers' Union.

1948   The UN Security Council creates the State of Israel.

1953   A number of Jewish doctors are accused of planning to murder prominent Soviet Leaders in what becomes known as the Doctors' Plot. Stalin is making arrangements to transfer all citizens of Jewish nationality to the Far East.

Death of Stalin.

1956   Khrushchev denounces Stalin's crimes at Twentieth Party Congress. Ehrenburg publishes his novel *The Thaw*. There is an uprising in Hungary which is put down with great severity.

1957   Pasternak's *Dr Zhivago* is published in Italy, and brings him worldwide fame.

1958	Nobel Prize offered to Pasternak, citing his poetry.
1960	Death of Pasternak.
1961	Yevgeny Yevtushenko writes his poem 'Babiy Yar' which expresses his horror at the massacre, and also at continuing anti-Semitism.
1964	Leonid Brezhnev succeeds Khrushchev, and tries to re-establish more central control. Trial of Joseph Brodsky.
1972	Joseph Brodsky deported from Soviet Union.
1975	Elaine Feinstein's first visit to Russia.
1978	Elaine Feinstein visits Russia as a guest of GB/USSR and the Writers' Union.
1982	Yuri Andropov rises from Head of the KGB to become first Secretary of the Party. He dies of kidney failure in 1984.
1985	Gorbachev succeeds Andropov as General Secretary of the Party, and institutes reforms to the Soviet system. Joseph Brodsky is awarded Nobel Prize.
1989	The Berlin Wall falls, and the Soviet Empire begins to collapse.
1991	A group of hard-line Communists attempt a military coup, which fails when the soldiers are unwilling to fire on the citizens of Moscow, who link hands against them. The Soviet Union is formally dissolved in December.
	Boris Yeltsin becomes the new leader of the Russian Federation.
	Elaine Feinstein visits Russia.
1998	Elaine Feinstein visits Russia while researching her biography of Pushkin.
	The Russian Federation is in economic crisis, with many salaries unpaid and savings destroyed by hyper-inflation.
1999	Boris Yeltsin resigns at the end of December, and leaves the presidency in the hands of Vladimir Putin.

2003 Elaine Feinstein visits Russia while researching her biography of Akhmatova.

2005 Elaine Feinstein visits Russia and the Ukraine.